Also by Enid Blyton

The Enchanted Wood
The Magic Faraway Tree
The Folk of the Faraway Tree
Up the Faraway Tree

Naughty Amelia Jane!
Amelia Jane is Naughty Again!
Amelia Jane gets into Trouble!
Amelia Jane Again!
Good Idea, Amelia Jane!

The Adventures of the Wishing-Chair
The Wishing-Chair Again
More Wishing-Chair Stories

The Mystery of the Burnt Cottage
The Mystery of the Disappearing Cat
The Mystery of the Secret Room
The Mystery of the Spiteful Letters
The Mystery of the Missing Necklace
The Mystery of the Hidden House
The Mystery of the Pantomime Cat
The Mystery of the Invisible Thief
The Mystery of the Vanished Prince
The Mystery of the Strange Bundle
The Mystery of Holly Lane
The Mystery of Tally-Ho Cottage
The Mystery of the Missing Man
The Mystery of the Strange Messages
The Mystery of Banshee Towers

Enid Blyton

ALL ABOARD!

EGMONT

EGMONT

We bring stories to life

The Saucy Jane Family first published in Great Britain 1948
The Pole Star Family and *The Seaside Family* first published in Great Britain 1950
The Queen Elizabeth Family first published in Great Britain 1951
This edition published 2014 by Egmont UK Limited
The Yellow Building, 1 Nicholas Road,
London W11 4AN

ISBN 978 1 4052 6905 6

A CIP catalogue record for this title is available from the British Library

Typeset by Avon DataSet Ltd, Bidford on Avon, Warwickshire
Printed and bound in Great Britain by the CPI Group

55940/1

MIX
Paper
FSC   FSC® C018306

EGMONT LUCKY COIN

Our story began over a century ago, when seventeen-year-old
Egmont Harald Petersen found a coin in the street.

He was on his way to buy a flyswatter, a small hand-operated
printing machine that he then set up in his tiny apartment.

The coin brought him such good luck that today Egmont has
offices in over 30 countries around the world. And that lucky
coin is still kept at the company's head offices in Denmark.

The
Saucy Jane
Family

Contents

1

A Most Exciting Idea

Mike, Belinda and Ann were three lucky children. They were at school all the week – and from Friday to Monday they lived in a caravan!

Mummy and Daddy lived in one caravan and the three children had the other. It was such fun. In the holidays they went to visit Uncle Ned and Aunt Clara. Then their two good horses, Davey and Clopper, pulled the caravans down many little winding lanes to Uncle Ned's farm.

'It's lovely to have a house on wheels!' cried Mike, when he sat at the front of his caravan and drove Clopper steadily on. 'I wouldn't like to live in a house that always stood still.'

When the summer holidays came, Daddy wondered whether they should all go to the sea. 'Our caravans want cleaning and painting,' he said. 'The stove wants something done to it, too.'

'Oh, Daddy – must we go and stay in a *house*!' said Ann, who, now that she had lived in a caravan on wheels, didn't like living in a house at all. 'Can't we take the caravans with us?'

'No. We really must get them properly cleaned up,' said Daddy. 'I'd like to take you to the sea, because you must learn to swim, and to handle a boat. All children should know how to swim.'

'I'd like to,' said Mike. 'I'd like to dive as well. And swim under water like a fish. I've seen people doing it.'

It was very difficult to get rooms by the sea anywhere, because Daddy had left it rather late. He tried to hire a caravan by the sea, too, but they were all taken. It really seemed as if the children wouldn't be able to go.

And then one day Mummy had a most exciting letter. She read it to herself first, and her eyes shone.

'Listen!' she said. 'I wonder how you would like this, children?'

'What?' cried the three of them, and Daddy looked up from his newspaper.

'It's a letter from an old friend of mine,' said Mummy. 'She has a houseboat on a canal not very far from here – and she says she will lend it to us for the holidays if we like.'

'A houseboat?' said Ann, in wonder. 'What's that? Does she mean a boat-house – where boats are kept?'

Everyone laughed. 'Isn't Ann a baby?' said Mike. 'Silly, it's a proper boat that people *live* in – they make their home there, just as we make ours in the caravan.'

'*Do* they?' said Ann. 'Do they really live on the boat all day and night? Oh Mummy, I'd like to see a houseboat.'

'And I'd simply LOVE to live in one!' said Belinda. 'Oh, I would! To hear the water all day and night, and to see fish jumping – and the little moorhens swimming about. Oh, Mummy!'

'Where's this houseboat?' said Daddy. 'It certainly does sound rather exciting.'

'It's at Mayberry,' said Mummy. 'On the canal there. It's a very pretty part, I know. It's a lovely houseboat – big enough to take all of us quite comfortably.'

'What's the boat called?' asked Mike. 'Does the letter say, Mummy?'

'Yes. It's called the *Saucy Jane*,' said Mummy, smiling. 'What a funny name!'

'It's a *lovely* name!' said Belinda. 'I like it. The *Saucy Jane*. We shan't be the Caravan Family – we shall be the Family of the *Saucy Jane*.'

'Let's go today,' said Ann. 'Mummy, can we?'

'Of course not,' said Mummy. 'You can't do things all in a hurry like that. Daddy has got to arrange about the caravans being done – and we must find out what we can do with Davey and Clopper.'

'Oh, Mummy – we can't leave Davey and Clopper behind,' cried Mike. 'You know we can't. They would be awfully miserable.'

'Well, we can't have horses living on a boat,' said

Daddy. 'Be sensible, Mike.'

'They could live in a nearby field,' said Mike. He loved Davey and Clopper with all his heart, and looked after them well.

'We'll see,' said Daddy. 'They might perhaps be useful to us if we wanted to go up the canal a little way in the houseboat.'

'Oh – would Davey and Clopper pull our boat?' cried Ann. 'Wouldn't they feel odd, pulling a boat instead of a caravan?'

'Well – what about it, Daddy?' said Mummy, still looking rather excited. 'Shall we try a holiday on a houseboat? The children could learn to swim and dive, and they could learn to handle a little boat too. Just what we want them to do.'

'It does seem as if we were meant to go,' said Daddy, smiling. 'We can't get in anywhere by the sea – so a river or a canal is the next best thing. Yes, write to your friend and tell her we'll go and see the *Saucy Jane*.'

'And we'll make up our minds whether to live in it for the holidays or not when we see it,' said Mummy.

'I'm going to tell Davey and Clopper all about it,' said Ann, and she ran off to where the two big horses stood close together in the field.

'Don't be long,' called Mummy. 'It's almost time to go to bed.'

But when they were in their bunks in the caravan that night, the three children couldn't go to sleep for a long time. They talked about the *Saucy Jane*, they planned what they would do – and when at last they did fall asleep they dreamt about her too.

The *Saucy Jane*! What would she be like? Just as nice as a caravan – perhaps nicer!

2

The *Saucy Jane*

Next morning at breakfast-time all the family talked about when they could go and see the *Saucy Jane*.

'The sooner the better, *I* think,' said Daddy. 'What about today? There's a bus that goes quite near Mayberry. We could catch it and walk across the fields to the canal.'

'Oh, Daddy – today!' said Belinda. 'Yes, let's go today. It's such a lovely day.'

So when they had washed up the breakfast things, tidied the caravans, and locked the doors, they all set off. They caught the bus at the corner of the lane and settled down for a fairly long ride.

'What is a canal, Daddy? Is it a river?' asked Ann.

'Oh, no,' said Daddy. 'A canal is made by man – cut out by machinery, and filled with water. It is usually very straight, but if it meets a hill it goes round it.'

'Doesn't it ever go through it?' asked Mike.

'Yes, sometimes. Some canals go through quite long tunnels,' said Daddy; 'a mile, two miles or more.'

'Do fishes live in canal water – and wild birds?' asked Belinda.

'Oh, yes,' said Daddy. 'They are old now, these canals we have made all over the country, and to you they will look just like rivers. They have weeds growing in them, fish of many kinds, wild birds on the banks. Trees lean over the sides, fields come right down to the canals, though where they run through towns there are houses by them, of course.'

'Why did we build canals, when we have so many rivers?' asked Mike.

'Well, many goods were sent by water in the old days, when goods had to be taken about all over the country, and the roads were bad, and the railways were only just beginning,' said Daddy. 'But rivers wind about too much – so straight canals were cut.'

'I see,' said Mike. 'I suppose big boats were loaded in the towns, and then they were taken across the country to other big towns – by canal.'

'Yes,' said Daddy. 'I'll show you the boats that take them – canal-boats and barges. You'll see plenty going by if we live on the houseboat.'

'*If!* You mean *when*!' cried Belinda. 'Are we nearly there, Daddy? I want to see the canal and the *Saucy Jane*. I can't wait another minute.'

But she had to wait, because the bus was not yet near Mayberry. At last it stopped at a little inn and the bus conductor called to Daddy.

'This is where you get out, sir. You'll find the canal across those fields there. You can just see it from here.'

They all got out. They climbed the stile and walked across a cornfield by a narrow path right through the middle of the whispering corn. The corn was as high as Ann, and she liked looking through the forest of tall green stalks.

They crossed another field and then came to the canal. It was, as Daddy had said, very like an ordinary river. Trees and bushes overhung the opposite side, but the cornfield went right down to the edge of the side they were on.

The canal stretched as far as they could see, blue and straight. A little way up it, on the opposite side, were two or three big white boats – houseboats, with people living in them. Smoke rose from the chimney of one of them.

'There are the boats,' said Mummy. 'I wonder which is the *Saucy Jane*! Dear me, Daddy, how are we going to get across?'

'Borrow a little boat and row it!' said Daddy. 'Come along!'

They were soon just opposite the houseboats. One was very colourful indeed, with red geraniums and blue lobelias planted in pots and baskets all round the sitting-space on the little roof.

'I do hope that's the *Saucy Jane*,' said Belinda to Ann. 'It's much the nicest. It's so shining white, too!'

There was a small cottage by the canal, and a woman was in the garden hanging out clothes. Daddy called to her. 'Is the *Saucy Jane* over there? Can we get to her in a boat?'

'Yes, that's the *Saucy Jane*,' said the woman. 'The boat with the geraniums. She's got a little boat belonging to her, but I expect it's moored beside her. You're welcome to borrow my boat, if you like. It's the little dinghy down beside you.'

'Thank you,' said Daddy.

Everyone got in, Daddy united the rope and took the oars. Over the water they went to the *Saucy Jane*. Somebody came out on deck, appearing from the cabin-part in the middle.

Mummy gave a cry of delight. 'Molly! You're here! We've come to see the boat!'

'Oh, what fun!' cried Mummy's friend. 'I never expected you so soon. Look, tie your dinghy just there – and climb up.'

In great excitement the children climbed up on the spotless deck. So this was the *Saucy Jane* – a house on a boat! They looked at the cabin-part; proper doors led into it, two doors, painted white with a little red line round the panels.

There were chairs on deck to sit in and watch the boats that went by. There were even chairs on the roof-part, up by the geraniums and lobelias. Ann didn't know which to do first – climb up on the roof by the little iron ladder, or go into the exciting-looking cabin.

'Come along and I'll show you over the *Saucy Jane*,' said Mummy's friend, smiling. 'You can call me Auntie Molly. When you've seen everything, we'll sit down and have some biscuits and lemonade, and talk about whether you'd like to have a holiday here.'

'We would, we would!' said all three children together. 'We've made up our minds already!'

3

What Fun to be on a Houseboat!

It was very exciting to explore the big houseboat. Down in the cabin-part there were two bedrooms and a small living-room. There was even a tiny kitchen, very clean and neat, with just room to take about two steps in!

In one room there was no bed, though Auntie Molly said it was a bedroom. In the other room there were bunks for beds, just as there were in the caravan – two on one side of the wall, and a third that could be folded up into the wall on the other side.

'I call that bunk my spare-room,' said Auntie Molly, with a laugh. 'I can sleep three people in this bedroom and two in the other.'

'But where do they sleep in the other room?' asked Mike, puzzled. 'I didn't see any bed at all.'

'Oh, I forgot to show it to you,' said Auntie Molly. 'It's really rather clever, the way it comes out of the wall. Come and see.'

She took them back into the other cabin bedroom, and went to the wall at the back. There was a handle there and she pulled it. Out came a double bed, opening itself like a concertina! Auntie Molly pulled down four short legs, and hey presto! there was the bed. Tucked away in another cupboard were blankets, sheets and mattress.

'It's like magic,' said Ann. 'And isn't it a good idea? It would take up a lot of room if you had the bed standing all day in this little room. Can I push it back, please?'

It was as easy to push back into the wall as it was to pull out.

'That will be Mummy's and Daddy's bed,' said Belinda. 'Auntie Molly, this houseboat is just right for our family, you know – you've got beds or bunks for five people.'

'Yes,' said Aunt Mollie. 'I knew you had been used to living in a caravan, and I thought you would be just the family to enjoy my houseboat. I was sure you would keep it clean and tidy, because I've heard how beautiful your caravans are.'

'Oh, yes – we'd keep your boat spotless,' said Belinda. 'I would scrub down the deck each day. I'd love that. That's what sailors do, isn't it, Mummy?'

There was a stove in the tiny kitchen for cooking, and a chimney stuck out at the top of the roof for the smoke. There were neat cupboards all round the kitchen, and mugs and cups hung in neat rows.

'You can wash up in the canal water,' said Aunt Mollie, 'and any other washing you want to do you can do in the canal too. Drinking-water you can get from Mrs Toms' well at the cottage opposite. I fetch it in a big water-jar.'

'I can see that our jobs here will be quite different from our jobs in the caravan,' said Mike, 'but they will be very exciting. Daddy, can I fetch the drinking-water each day, please?'

'As soon as you can handle a boat, and can swim, you may,' said Daddy.

Aunt Molly suddenly looked rather alarmed. 'Oh – can't the children swim?' she said. 'Then I really don't think you ought to come and live here. You see, it's so easy to fall into the water, and if you can't swim, you might drown.'

The children stared at her in dismay. How dreadful if they couldn't come and live on this lovely boat just because they couldn't swim!

'We're going to learn,' said Mike at once. 'We're going to learn the very first day we get here. You needn't worry.'

'But can the little girl learn?' asked Aunt Molly, looking doubtfully at Ann. 'Really, I think if you come you'll have to tie her up with a rope, so that if she does fall into the water she can drag herself back to the houseboat.'

'Tie me up? Like a little dog? I won't be tied up!' cried Ann indignantly. 'I've never heard of such a thing!'

'My dear child, a great many of the canals-people tie their children up until they can swim,' said Aunt Molly. 'Now, just look what's coming by. I believe it's a canal-boat called *Happy Sue*. If it is you will see the two babies of the *Happy Sue* tied up with ropes. How could their parents possibly risk letting them fall in and be drowned?'

A long canal-boat came chugging by. In the middle of it was a built-up cabin, where the people lived. In the hold, where they carried goods, were great boxes which the boat was taking to the next big town. On these boxes played two small children, about two years old. They were so alike that the children guessed they were twins.

'Yes – they are tied to that post by a rope,' said Belinda, in surprise. 'Oh, Aunt Molly, what a pretty boat – it's all painted with castles and roses.'

'All the canal-boats are painted like that,' said Aunt Molly. 'The canal-people have their own ways and customs. You must make friends with some of the children and let them tell you all about their unusual life. They are always on the move, sailing up and down the canals they know so well.'

The canal-boat went by, and behind it were two barges full of coal, which the first boat was pulling along. The *Saucy Jane* bobbed up and down a little as the big boats went by and sent waves rippling to the banks.

'Oh! – now the *Saucy Jane* really *does* feel like a boat!' said Ann, delighted. 'She was so still before, she might have been on land. But now she's bobbing like a real boat. I like it.'

'Now for biscuits and lemonade,' said Aunt Molly. 'And we'll decide when you're to come. I move out tomorrow. You can come any time after that.'

'The very next day!' shouted Mike. 'Mummy, can we? The very next day!'

And Mummy nodded her head. 'Yes, we'll come on Thursday. We really will.'

4

Settling In

The children went back to their caravans in great excitement. It really seemed too good to be true, to think that they were actually going to the *Saucy Jane* on Thursday!

Daddy went to see a man in the village about painting and cleaning the caravans. A nearby farmer asked if he might borrow Davey for the holidays, to help in the harvesting. He didn't want Clopper.

'Yes, you may certainly borrow Davey,' said Daddy. 'He's getting too fat. He could do with some hard work. We will take Clopper with us, in case we want to go up the canal in the *Saucy Jane*.'

On Thursday a car drew up in the lane outside the field where the two caravans stood. Mummy and the children got into it with their luggage. Daddy said goodbye to them, standing by big Clopper, who looked in surprise at the waving family.

'It's all right, Clopper. Daddy is riding you all the way to the *Saucy Jane!*' called Ann. 'You'll take longer than we do. We'll have everything ready for you, Daddy, when you come.'

Off went the car. Daddy jumped up on Clopper's broad back, and the two jogged off down the lane. Daddy knew some short cuts, but even so it would take a long while to get to Mayberry on slow old Clopper. But who minded that on this lovely summer's day, when honeysuckle grew in the hedges, and red poppies glowed in the corn! Daddy felt very happy, and he whistled as he rode on Clopper, thinking of the *Saucy Jane*, and wondering how his little family would like their new life.

'The very first thing I must do is to teach them all to swim,' he thought. 'Ann doesn't like the water very much. I do hope she won't make a fuss about it. I wonder if they have reached the *Saucy Jane* yet.'

They had! They were even then climbing up on her spotless deck, calling happily to one another.

'Here we are, in our new home! I hope lots of boats and barges go by so that the *Saucy Jane* bobs up and down all the time!'

'I'm going to have the top bunk. Mummy, can I have the top one? I like climbing.'

'I'll always pull your bed out of the wall, Mummy, and get it ready for you at night.' That was Belinda. She loved to be useful. Living in a caravan and having to do so many odd jobs had taught her to be a very sensible little girl indeed.

Auntie Molly had left blankets, linen, crockery, knives and forks – in fact, everything they would

21

need. Mummy said that it was even more important to keep Auntie Molly's things nice than their own.

'It is so very kind of her to lend them to us and to trust us with them,' she said. 'We must be extra careful not to break anything, or spoil any of her belongings. If people trust us, the least we can do is to be trustworthy!'

It was such fun unpacking their things and putting them into the drawers that lined the walls of the little cabin-bedrooms. There was even space to hang coats and dresses. Belinda went on shore to pick some flowers to fill the vase on the little table in the sitting-room.

Mummy began to cook a meal on the small stove. She had already packed away into the neat larder the food they had brought with them. She was used to the ways of a caravan, where every bit of space was used. It was just the same on the houseboat.

Soon the smell of bacon frying filled the air, and the children sniffed hungrily.

'Where's Daddy? Isn't he coming yet?' said Ann, and she went out on the deck.

Mummy called to her warningly.

'Now, Ann – don't go near the edge of the boat, in case you topple over! You're not tied up, you know.'

'I can see Daddy and Clopper!' shouted Ann. 'Mike! Belinda! Here he comes! Look at old Clopper; he's as proud as anything to carry Daddy. Hi, Daddy, DADDY!'

Daddy had arranged with Mrs Toms to let Clopper stay in a little field opposite the boat, where she kept a cow and a few geese. He jumped down from the big horse's back, called to Mrs Toms, gave Clopper a friendly smack and ran to the little dinghy by the bank. Clopper stared after him. 'Hrrrrumph!' he said, in surprise, as he saw Daddy rowing off in the boat. Then he went down to the water to have a long drink.

'Hallo, Daddy!' called the children. 'You're just in time for supper. Can you smell the bacon?'

'Welcome to the *Saucy Jane*!' said Mummy, appearing out of the cabin door, her face red with cooking. 'Shall we have our meal up on deck? The cabin is very tiny, and it's such a lovely evening.'

'Oh, yes, yes,' said Belinda. 'I know where a little folding table is. I'll get it and lay it. Hurrah for supper on deck!'

Very soon they were all sitting round the low table, enjoying their first meal on the *Saucy Jane*. A little breeze ran over the water, and the boat lifted herself up and down on the ripples. Two moorhens swam by, and a fish suddenly jumped right out of the water at a fly. Swallows flew low, just skimming the canal, twittering in their sweet high voices.

'This is the loveliest place in the world,' said Belinda. 'Lovelier than the caravan. Oh, listen to the plash-plash of the water against the sides of the boat, Mummy.'

'I do love being right at the very beginning of a holiday,' said Ann, sleepily. 'It's such a nice feeling. I don't want to go to bed tonight, Mummy. I want to stay up on deck for hours and hours and hours.'

'Well, it's your bedtime now,' said Mummy. 'Hurry, and you can have the top bunk! It may be nice out here – but think of sleeping down there, with the *Saucy Jane* bobbing whenever a boat goes by. Hurry, Ann. You're half asleep already!'

5

Belinda Wakes Up Early

The first day on the *Saucy Jane* was one long delight.
Belinda awoke first and crept out of her bunk so as
not to wake the others. She went up on deck in her
nightie, but it was already so warm that she was not
a bit cold.

The canal stretched up and down, a soft pale blue,
edged with green. The sun was rising, and here
and there gold flecks freckled the water. The two
moorhens swam by again, and a magnificient swan
floated slowly up, his image reflected so beautifully
in the water that he really almost looked like two
swans, Belinda thought.

'One swan the right way up and the other upside
down,' she said to herself. 'Swan, come back at
breakfast-time and I'll give you some bread.'

The swan turned his head on his long, graceful
neck, gave Belinda a look, and then sailed on again.
The swallows came down to the water for flies,
twittering all the time. Belinda leaned over to look
down into the water itself.

'There are hundreds and hundreds of baby fish!'

she said. 'All going about together. How they dart about! And there's a great big fish. He's made all the little ones hurry away. Oh, here comes a canal-boat.'

The gaily-painted boat slid along – but this time it had no motor inside it to chug-chug-chug and send it through the water. Instead, to Belinda's great delight, a big horse was pulling it.

The horse walked steadily along a path on the opposite bank. A rope tied to him ran to the boat, and by this he pulled the long, heavy boat along. A girl sat by the long tiller, guiding her boat easily.

She called to Belinda, 'Nice morning! Going to be hot today!'

'I wish we lived on a boat like yours!' called Belinda. 'Ours stays still.'

'Yours is only a houseboat,' cried the girl. 'It's a play-boat. Ours goes to work. It's a canal-boat. We go for miles and miles. Goodbye!'

The canal-boat slid right by, sending waves to make the *Saucy Jane* bob again. The horse pulling the boat had not even turned his head. Belinda could hear the sound of his hoofs for a long time in the clear still morning air.

Mummy had heard her calling, and woke up. She looked at her little clock. Half-past five in the morning! Whatever was Belinda doing, up so early? Mummy went up on deck, ready to scold.

'Belinda,' she began in a low voice, 'do you know

that it's only half-past five? How naughty of you to come up here and shout!'

'Mummy – it's so perfectly lovely,' said Belinda, putting her arm round her mother. 'Other people are awake. Look, that long boat has just passed by and the little girl guiding it called out to me. And here comes another boat – without a horse this time, but with a motor inside to drive it. Chug-chug-chug – it makes rather a nice noise, I think.'

Mummy forgot to scold. She sat there in the early morning sunshine with Belinda, watching everything. The water was a deeper blue now, and the golden patches were so bright that Belinda could not look at them.

The big fish went flashing by. More and more flies danced over the water and the swallows skimmed along by the dozen, snapping up the flies for their breakfast. The magnificent swan came back again, and looked at Belinda as if to say, 'Is it breakfast-time yet?'

'Not nearly,' said Belinda. 'Though I'm most awfully hungry.'

Mummy laughed. 'I believe I can hear the others waking up,' she said. 'If so, we'd better all get up and I'll get breakfast. We can always have a sleep in the afternoon if we are tired. But really, this morning is too beautiful to waste even a minute of it.'

Ann and Mike came up on deck, rubbing their

sleepy eyes. Ann cried out in joy when she saw the sparkling water and the waiting swan.

'Oh, you should have woken me too! Mummy, isn't it lovely to know there's water under us, not land? Oh, do let's feed the swan. Where's Daddy? Daddy, wake up! You're missing something lovely!'

Then Daddy too came out in surprise, and sat down to watch the water and the swan and the fish. They all watched the long canal-boats too, painted with so many bright patterns. Even the drinking-jars were painted, and the kettles and saucepans.

Some of the smaller children were tied with ropes, and once the children saw a dog on a barge, tied up with a rope too.

'He might fall in without being noticed,' said Daddy, 'and though he can swim, he would soon be left behind. So they've tied him up.'

'Good morning to you!' called the canal-people politely, as they passed in their long boats, and each time the *Saucy Jane* bobbed as if she too was saying good morning.

'How early the canal-folk go to work,' said Mummy. 'I suppose they are up at sunrise and in bed at sunset. Well, if *we* get up at sunrise like this, our bedtime will have to be early too. Get dressed, children, and I'll cook breakfast. You lay the table, Belinda, and we'll have it out here.'

It was a very early breakfast, but the children

thought it was the nicest one they had ever had. The swan came up to be fed, and pecked up the bits of bread from the water. Once or twice he caught them in his beak when Mike threw some, and the children thought this was very clever.

'Well – we must get on with a few jobs,' said Mummy at last. 'And then, my dears, you are going to have a most important lesson. Daddy's going to teach you how to swim!'

6

A Most Important Lesson

The children hurried to do the little jobs on the boat. Belinda helped Mummy to wash up. The dishes were put into the rack to dry. Belinda had to give them a polish with a cloth when she laid the table.

Ann made the beds, or rather the bunks. Mike took out all the bedding from his mother's bed, folded it tidily and put it into its cupboard. Then back into the wall went the bed, folding up neatly.

Daddy went to see if Clopper was all right, and to do a little shopping. Everyone worked happily. It didn't seem to be work, somehow! The sun shone down warmly, and the water glittered and sparkled. The swan sailed about round the boat hopefully, and drove away the two moorhens.

'I wish Daddy would come back,' said Ann. 'I want to swim across to the other side.'

'You won't be able to swim at once, silly,' said Mike. 'It may take you a few days to learn. Look, lie flat on the deck, and I'll show you the strokes to use with your arms and legs.'

But before Ann could do that, Daddy hailed

them from the shore. 'Just coming! Are you ready for a swim?'

He was soon across and changed into swimming trunks. 'Now,' he said, 'I'm going to dive into the water and swim past the boat. I want you all to lean over and watch how I use my arms and legs. I shall use my arms like this . . . they will push away the water in front of me, and my legs will open and shut, so that I drive my body through the water. You must all watch carefully.'

Splash! Daddy dived beautifully into the canal, and the children watched him. They could see his brown arms and legs moving strongly.

'I see how he swims,' said Ann. 'Look, he pushes away the water with his arms, and brings them back in front of him to begin all over again, and he opens and shuts his legs like a frog does when *he* swims. I'm sure I could do that!'

Mike was watching very closely. He lay down flat on the deck. 'Watch me, Mummy,' he said, and he began to do the same arm and leg strokes as Daddy. 'Am I doing it right? Are these the strokes I should use?'

'Yes, Mike. That looks very good,' said Mummy. 'If only you can do that in the water, you'll do well. You lie down and do the strokes too, Ann and Belinda.'

So they did, but Mummy said they were not as good as Mike. Then Daddy called to them. 'Get on to the bank, and you'll find a nice shallow piece of water to step into. It will only be up to your waists, and you can learn your strokes there.'

The three children climbed on to the bank. Then they slid down into the water. They were hot with the sun and the water was cold.

'Oooh!' said Mike, but he plunged himself right under at once. That was what Daddy always did, he knew.

'Oooh!' said Belinda, and waited a bit. She went in very slowly, bit by bit, not liking the cold water very much but determined to be brave.

'Good girl! Jolly good, Mike!' cried Daddy. 'Come on, Ann!'

But Ann wouldn't go in any further than her knees. 'It's cold!' she kept saying. 'It's too cold!'

'It's warm once you're in!' cried Mike. 'Baby Ann! Doesn't like the cold water! How can you learn to swim if you don't even get in?'

'Go on, Ann,' said Mummy, who was now in the water herself, swimming along strongly. 'Hurry up! You look silly, shivering there.'

It took Ann at least ten minutes to get in up to her waist. Daddy and Mummy began to teach Mike and Belinda, and they took no more notice of Ann.

'If she wants to be a baby, we'll let her,' said Daddy. 'Now, Mike, that's right – out with your arms – bring them back – out again. Good! Now try your legs. I'll put my hand under your tummy and hold you safe so that you won't go under. You can trust me. I'll be sure to tell you when I think you're doing well enough to take my hand away.'

Mike got on extremely well. Soon Daddy took his hand away from under his tummy, and to his great delight Mike found that he could swim three strokes all by himself without going under.

'You'll soon be able to swim,' said Daddy, pleased, and turned to see how Mummy was getting on with Belinda. She too was doing her best, and Mummy was pleased with her. But she would not let Mummy take her hand away, so they couldn't tell if she could really swim a few strokes or not.

As for Ann, she wouldn't even try! As soon as Daddy made her take her legs off the bottom of the canal, she screamed, 'Don't! Don't! I'm frightened!'

'Well, you needn't be,' said Mike. 'Daddy won't let you go. You can trust him.'

But Ann was silly and she wouldn't even try to use her arms in the way Daddy told her. So he sent her back to the boat.

'I'm ashamed of you,' he said. 'You must try again tomorrow.'

After a while they all got out of the water and lay on the warm roof of the cabin to dry themselves in the sun. It was delicious! Ann felt rather ashamed of herself.

'I'll try properly tomorrow,' she told Daddy. 'I really will.'

'Well, little Ann, you can see for yourself that if you live on the water you must know how to swim,' said Daddy. 'I'll give you another chance tomorrow, and we'll see how you get on. Mike and Belinda will be swimming in a week's time – you don't want to be the only person in the *Saucy Jane* Family who can't swim, do you?'

7

Ann Has a Dreadful Shock

The happy summer days went by, and soon the family felt as if they had been living on the *Saucy Jane* for weeks! The weather was hot, the canal was blue and silver from dawn to dusk, and the swan became so tame that he hardly ever left the boat, but bobbed about by it all day. All night too, Belinda said, for once when she had gone on deck in the middle of the night she had seen him sleeping nearby, his head tucked under his wing.

Mike and Belinda could swim well now. Mike especially was a fine strong swimmer, and Daddy was proud of him. But Ann was still foolish. She squealed when she first went into the water and always made a fuss. And she wouldn't try to swim at all.

But one afternoon something happened that made her change her mind. Mummy was lying down in the cabin, glad to be out of the blazing sun. Daddy had gone to talk to a fisherman up the canal. Mike and Belinda were on the bank at the back of the houseboat, lying in the cool grass.

Ann was playing with Stella, one of her best-loved

dolls. And quite suddenly Stella slid along the deck and fell overboard into the water.

Ann gave a squeal. 'Oh, Stella! Don't drown! Keep still and I'll reach you with a stick!'

She got a stick and, leaning over the edge of the boat, she tried to hook poor Stella up to safety. But instead of doing that, she found herself slipping too, and suddenly into the water she went with a splash! She screamed as she fell, 'Mike! Mike!' Then she could say no more, for she went right under the water and sank down, choking. She struck out with her arms, but she had not learnt to swim, and she was terrified.

'Why didn't I learn, why didn't I learn?' she thought, as she went down deeper. Water poured into her nose and mouth, she couldn't breathe, she couldn't do anything at all!

Mike heard the shout. He shot up from the bank when he heard the splash. He ran on to the boat, looked over the edge and saw poor Ann sinking down into the canal.

'MUMMY!' yelled Mike. 'Ann's fallen in!'

Then the plucky boy jumped straight into the canal himself and tried to reach Ann. He found her, and tried to pull her up. In a terrible fright the little girl clutched him, and began to pull him down under the water too.

Goodness knows what would have happened

next if Mummy hadn't gone into the water too, and somehow got the two of them into the shallow part, where Mike could stand. He was gasping and choking. 'Oh Mummy, she nearly drowned me.'

Mummy carried Ann up on deck. The little girl's eyes were closed, but she was breathing. She had not been in the water long enough for any great harm to be done. She soon opened her eyes, choked, and began to cry with fright.

Mummy was very frightened about Ann's fall.

'We daren't risk such a thing happening again,' she said to Daddy, who was very upset too. 'She won't learn to swim, so we shall just *have* to tie her to a rope.'

Then, much to Ann's dismay, she had a rope tied round her waist all the time she was on the boat. Now, if she fell into the water, she could haul herself out. But Ann hated the rope round her.

'The canal-boat children laugh at me,' she wept. 'Nobody as old as I am is tied up. I feel like a puppy-dog. Untie me Mummy, and I promise not to fall in again.'

'I'm sorry, darling, but we can't risk it,' said Mummy. 'You're too precious. And, after all, you can always get rid of the rope yourself, if you want to.'

'How?' asked Ann. 'I can't untie this big knot.'

'I know,' said Mummy. 'I don't mean that. I mean that you have only to be sensible and learn to swim and you will have the rope taken off at once.'

'Oh!' said Ann, and she began to think seriously about learning to swim. After all, it had been dreadful sinking down into the water and choking like that. She shivered whenever she thought of it. And it did seem easy to learn to swim if only she would be brave and trust Daddy.

'How can you be brave if you aren't?' she asked Mike.

'I don't know,' said Mike. 'You might put it into your prayers, perhaps. You can always ask God for help in anything, Mummy says.'

So that night Ann begged God in her prayers to help her to be brave enough to learn to swim, and made up her mind that she really would try.

And, of course, the very next day she found that once she let Daddy really help her, it wasn't so dreadful after all! She *could* be brave, she *could* try – and soon, she would be able to swim!

Daddy was pleased with her. 'You're just as brave as the others now,' he told her. 'And I do believe that you'll swim as fast as Belinda. You've got such a strong stroke with your legs. That's right – *shoot* your arms out – *use* your legs well. My word, I can hardly keep up with you!'

Ann was pleased. 'I did what you said, Mike, and asked God to help me,' she told him. 'It was much easier after that. I'll soon be able to swim as fast as you!'

Soon she was like a fish in the water, and Daddy

said she needn't have the rope tied round her any more. The whole family went swimming together, and presently Ann could actually swim right to the other bank, have a little rest and swim back again!

'I've a family of fish!' said Daddy. 'Now look out for waves – here come two barges!'

The children liked the waves. They lifted their arms from the water and hailed the barges, and the barge people shouted back.

'I wish we could go up the canal on a canal-boat,' said Ann. 'Oh, I really do wish we could.'

'Well, perhaps we can,' said Daddy. 'We'll have to find out!'

8

What Happened to Beauty

Daddy had decided that it wouldn't be possible to go up the canal on the heavy old houseboat, which was moored flat to the bank. The children had been very disappointed.

'We needn't have brought Clopper then,' said Ann. 'He won't have anything to do. He'll be very bored.'

'Well, maybe we can go on a canal-boat if we can find someone who will take us just for the trip,' said Daddy.

But somehow it didn't seem to happen. Either the boats were taking coal, and Mummy said she didn't want them to go on a dirty coalboat – or the canal-people didn't want to take them – or they just wouldn't stop long enough to discuss it.

Then one early morning a very strange thing happened just by the *Saucy Jane*. The children were all sitting on the houseboat roof watching the canal. They were waiting for a brilliant blue kingfisher who had fished near there the last day or two.

'He sits on that branch, watches for a fish, then dives straight into the water and catches it,' said

Mike. 'He's got such a strong beak.'

It was while they were watching for the kingfisher that the strange accident happened.

A canal-boat, drawn by a slow old horse, came silently up the canal. A boy was guiding the boat, yawning sleepily. No one walked beside the horse, which plodded along the tow-path by itself, its head down.

'Even the horse looks half asleep,' said Belinda. 'He stumbles a bit now and again, look.'

They watched the tired horse – and then, unexpectedly, it left the tow-path and walked straight into the water! It had fallen asleep as it walked, and in its sleep had not known where it was going.

It went in with a terrific splash! Mike leapt to his feet, startled. The boy on the canal-boat gave a yell. 'Dad! Beauty's fallen in. DAD!'

Then there was such a to-do! People poured up from the cabin of the canal-boat. The boat was guided towards where the horse was struggling in the canal.

'Oh, can he swim, can he swim?' squealed Ann. 'Oh, don't let him drown!'

But the horse had fortunately fallen into a shallow part of the water, and after he had lain in surprise on the mud, wide awake with shock, he decided to get up.

He was very frightened, and it took three of the canal-boatmen to quieten him and take him from the water. They rubbed him down, and one of them fixed a bag of oats on his nose. When he felt it there, he snuffled down into the oats and began to eat. Then the men knew he would be all right.

The children had watched the whole thing in the greatest excitement. Fancy a horse falling asleep and walking into the water! What a good thing he was all right.

The canal-boat was drawn up to the side. Everyone waited for the horse to recover himself and go on with his towing. But when he was set on the path again and coaxed to walk along it, he limped badly.

'Wait a minute,' said one of the men, and bent to examine the horse's leg. 'He's strained this leg. He won't be able to walk for a day or two, poor thing. It will never get better if we make him work now.'

'Well, what about our load?' said another man, impatiently. 'We've got to get that up to Birmingham before Saturday. It's important.'

'We'll get a tug to tow us,' said the first man.

Then Daddy, who had been listening and watching too, thought of a grand idea, and he called to the man.

'Hi! Do you want the loan of a good strong horse? I've got mine in the field there. You're welcome to use him for a bit if you like. He's longing for a bit of work.'

The men pushed their boat out from the side, and soon she was lying by the *Saucy Jane*. Daddy and the men began to talk. The children looked with the greatest interest at the long canal-boat.

'Look at all the castles and hearts and roses painted on the sides of the boat,' said Mike. 'We've often seen them before, but we've never been able to look at them so closely as this. I wonder who painted them and why.'

'All the canal-boats have them,' said Belinda. 'I wish I could get on this boat and look at everything. Even the tiller is painted, Mike. Just look.'

'I say – listen to what Daddy is saying,' said Mike suddenly, in excitement.

'Well,' Daddy was saying, 'you are welcome to borrow Clopper, my horse, if you like, and leave yours to rest in the field over there. He's a good strong horse, is Clopper.'

'That's kind of you, sir,' said the old boatman. 'Er – how much would you be asking us for the use of him?'

'Oh, I don't want you to pay me anything,' said Daddy. 'I'd be glad to have my horse getting a bit of exercise.'

'Well, sir – I don't rightly like taking your horse and giving nothing back,' said the old man.

'Would you like to do something for *me*, then?' said Daddy, and he smiled. 'See those three youngsters of mine? They badly want to go up the canal for a trip – but this houseboat of ours won't budge. You wouldn't like to take us with you, would you?'

'Ay, that I would, if you don't mind putting up with our rough ways,' said the old boatman. 'We'll be going through a few locks, and the children will like to see those at work. And we'll be passing through a long tunnel too, bored in a big hill.'

'Daddy, can we really go?' cried Belinda, and she rushed up to her father. 'It would be grand. I *do* so want to travel up the canal and see everything.'

'Well, just for a day,' said Daddy. 'We'll be ready in ten minutes, boatman. You can go and get my horse while you're waiting!'

9

A Day on the *Happy Ted*

Mummy quickly got ready a picnic meal to take with them, and told the children to get their macks just in case they needed them. The old boatman and his son went across to the field to get Clopper. Clopper came back with them willingly.

'I'm sure Clopper must feel as pleased and excited as we do!' said Ann. 'I shall take Stella. She'll want to see everything too.'

'I feel just like an adventure today,' said Mike. 'Goodness, fancy going up the canal – past villages and towns, through fields and woods, locks and tunnels!'

Clopper was tied to the tow-rope. The other horse, patted and petted, was left to graze peacefully in Clopper's field, and get over his shock. Everyone went on to the canal-boat.

One of the men went to walk with Clopper, for he had never been a tow-horse in his life. But he seemed to understand quite well exactly what to do, and he plodded along slowly and steadily.

The three children felt a little shy on the canal-boat at first. There was an old, rather fierce-looking woman there, but when she smiled she looked very kind. There were also three children, two boys and a girl, but they too seemed shy and hid among the boxes and crates that formed the cargo of the boat.

'It's called *Happy Ted*,' said Mike, reading the name painted on the boat.

'Happy Ted was my grandad,' said the old boatman. 'He got this boat and my granny on the same day, and he called it *Happy Ted* after himself. Then my father had it, and now I've got it. And my son there will have it one day.'

'Who paints all those lovely pictures everywhere?' asked Belinda, looking at the pretty castles and roses she saw on everything. 'I do like them.'

'Oh, I painted most of them,' said the old man. 'And my son he painted a few. All us canal-boat people paint our boats with hearts and castles and roses. It's our custom, and a very old one too.'

'You've painted your big water-can, and your kettles, and this biscuit-tin too,' said Ann. 'And you've even painted a pattern down the handle of your broom and your mop!'

'Ah, we like everything to be bright and tidy,' said the boatman's wife. 'You should see my cabin.'

'Can I?' said Ann, who was longing to peep into the tiny place where all the family seemed to live.

The old woman went backwards down the steps into the cabin. The children followed. There was hardly room for them to stand there all together, and certainly Daddy would have had to bend his head or he would have knocked it against the low ceiling.

But what a bright, lovely, little place it was! So tiny – like a dolls' house – and yet so many things in it that the children felt if they looked for hours they would never see them all.

There were a lot of brass knobs and ornaments hanging by the door. These glinted and winked like the sun, they were so bright and well-polished. Ann fingered one of them. 'It's like a brass ornament that Clopper wears,' she said. 'Why do you have so many?'

'Ah, we canal-folk collect them,' said the old woman. 'We like to see those brass things winking at us there. The better-off we are, the more we have. Don't you have any at home?'

'No,' said Ann, making up her mind to collect as many as she could, and hang them just inside her caravan door when she got back to it at the end of the holidays. 'Oh, look, Belinda, there's the little stove for cooking – and a table to sit at – but where's the bed?'

The bed was let into the wall in exactly the same way as the one in the *Saucy Jane*. On the wooden panel that shut it in was painted a bright pattern of hearts and roses. Mike wished he could paint like that. Perhaps Mummy would let him paint castles and things on the caravan door when he went back.

Everything was squashed into the small space of the cabin. The children could hardly believe that five or six people lived there all their lives!

'Fancy! You have your dinner here, and you sleep here, and on wet days you sit here!' said Mike. 'It must be a dreadful squeeze.'

'We like it,' said the old woman. 'I couldn't live in a house! What, be in a place that stands still all the time – that never hears the lap of the water, nor feels the swing of the waves! No, the canal-life's a grand life. We're water-wanderers, we are. You'll find us all up and down the canals, with our boats painted with hearts and roses and castles. We know the countryside like no one else, we know the canals and their ways, and we're proud of it!'

She looked at the children as if she was sorry for people who didn't live on a canal-boat. Land-folk! Poor things! What a boring life they must have, she thought.

It was hot and stuffy down in the little cabin, and Ann began to pant. They all went up the steps and out on deck. The long canal-boat was going smoothly through the water, with Clopper tugging her steadily.

'Good horse that,' said the old man, taking his pipe out of his mouth. 'Ay, a fine horse. He'll go a good many miles a day.'

The children gazed ahead, and saw that the country rose uphill in front of them.

'How can we get the boat uphill?' asked Belinda, puzzled. 'Look, we've got to go quite a long way up.'

'We'll go through a lock soon,' said the old boatman, smiling. 'Then you'll see how a boat can go uphill! Ah, you didn't know such a thing could be, did you? But you'll see, you'll see!'

10

Uphill in a Boat!

How can a boat go uphill? That was the question all the children were asking each other. Ann and Belinda did not know what a lock was, and Mike had only heard of canal-locks once or twice.

The *Happy Ted* went on and on, and Clopper's hoofs sounded just like his name as he plodded along. Then the old boatman pointed ahead.

'There's the lock,' he said. 'I'll tell you what happens, if you listen well.'

The children were all ears at once.

'Now you see,' said the old man, 'the water above the lock is higher than below it. How are we going to get the boat up to the higher water?'

The children couldn't imagine. 'Well, now,' said the old man, 'a lock is a small space, big enough to take one or two boats, between the high canal-water and the low canal-water. There are gates at each end, so that when a boat is in that bit of space, and both the gates are shut, she's sort of *locked* in. See?'

'Yes,' said the three.

'Well, now,' said the old man again, 'the gates at

our end, the low-water end, are open, and we'll go straight into that bit of space there. Then we'll shut the gates behind us and lock ourselves in.'

'What's the use of that?' asked Mike.

'Ah, you wait!' said the boatman. 'Now comes the clever bit! As soon as we're in that locked-up space, we're going to open holes in the gate in front of us. See? And water is going to pour through the holes, down into our locked-up bit of space. And that water is going to fill up the lock, and raise us up higher and higher and higher!'

'But what will happen when the water down in the lock rises as high as the water outside the gate?' said Mike.

'Aha! That's another clever bit!' said the boatman. 'What do we do then but open the gates in front of us and there we are, on a level with the high-up canal, and we can sail out as easy as you like!'

'It's a marvellous idea!' said Mike. 'Really marvellous! Oh, I do want to get into the lock and see it all happen!'

'But what do you do if you're in a boat that's coming down from a high part of the canal to the low part?' said Belinda.

'Easy!' said Mike. '*I* know that! You just go into the filled-up lock, shut the gates behind you, and then open holes in the opposite gate to let the water out and wait till the level of the lock is the same as the low part; then open the gates and out you go!'

'Right!' said the boatman. 'Now you watch what happens in a minute.'

Clopper walked right up to the lock. There was a steep bit of gravel for him to go up to the higher lock-gate, and up he went. The lower gates of the lock were open, and in went the *Happy Ted*.

She stayed there, held by the tow-rope, which was now fastened round a big stone. The gates behind her were shut by the boatman's son. Then he and the old boatman went to open the holes in the gate in front – the 'paddles,' as they were called.

The children sat in the *Happy Ted*, shut up in the lock, waiting. Above them, behind other tall gates, was a great high wall of water. Somehow they had to get the *Happy Ted* up there so that they might sail out on the level again.

Water began to pour into the lock through the paddles of the gate. What a noise it made! It was like waterfalls, rushing and gushing. The children felt excited.

'We're rising up, we're rising up! The lock is filling!' cried Belinda. 'See that mark on the wall above us – now it's level with us – now it's below us, lost in the water. We're rising up, we're rising up!'

The lock was filled at last. The *Happy Ted* was much higher up than she had been before. She was level with the high part of the canal. She nosed against the top parts of the lockgate and they swung open. Out she went, drawn by Clopper, who was now once more pulling hard on the tow-rope.

'We're through the lock! We're through! We've taken a boat uphill!' cried Mike. 'It's wonderful! Are there any more locks soon?'

'Oh, yes – there's plenty just here,' said the old man. 'It's slow work, going through them. But if you're not in a hurry, why worry?'

'We're not in a hurry! We'd like this day to last for a whole week!' said Ann. 'Oh, look at those corn-fields! They're getting golden already.'

The canal-boat went slowly on through fields and woods, past pretty gardens, past lonely farmhouses. Sometimes it went by a small village where children came to wave. Once or twice it came again to a lock, and the children this time got out to help to open and shut the gates. It was lovely to watch the water pouring fast into the lock, filling it, bringing the *Happy Ted* higher and higher, until at last she could sail proudly out on the level again, much higher up than she had been before.

They went slowly by a dirty town. Here the canal was muddy and smelt nasty. The children didn't like it.

'Do people *have* to live in towns?' asked Ann. 'Do they choose to?'

'Oh, lots of people don't like the country,' said

Daddy. 'I'm glad you love it. Look at that busy yard over there. See the loads being put into the canal-boats, swung into them by the big cranes.'

'How useful the boats are!' said Belinda, in wonder. 'What a lot of heavy things they carry, Daddy. There are rail-roads and ordinary roads, and water-roads, aren't there? But I like the water-roads the best.'

Out beyond the town they went, and in the distance stood a big hill. The canal ran straight towards it.

'We're going inside that hill,' said the boatman. 'Put on your macks. It's cold and wet in there.'

11

A Strange Adventure

'We've taken this boat uphill – and now we're going to take it *through* a hill,' said Belinda. 'It all sounds like magic. I never knew things like this happened before.'

'What happens to Clopper?' said Ann, suddenly. 'He won't like walking through a tunnel. He'll be afraid.'

'Oh, Clopper can't walk through the tunnel, missy,' said the boatman. 'There's no towpath. He'll have to go right over the hill. My son will take him.'

'Are you sure you children want to go through the tunnel?' said Mummy. 'You may be afraid. It's so dark and damp.'

But all the children meant to go. What, miss an adventure like this? Certainly not!

'How's the boat going to get through the tunnel without Clopper?' said Mike. 'It hasn't got a motor to drive it along, like a motor-boat.'

'There's a power-boat coming up behind,' said the boatman. 'He'll give us a tug. We'll wait for him. You take Clopper, son!' he called. His son leapt ashore, untied the tow-rope, and disappeared up a steep grassy path with Clopper. Ann pictured them walking right over the hill and down.

The power-boat came up. ' 'Hoy there!' called the boatman. 'Give us a tug, will you?'

'Right!' called back the other man, and went on ahead. He caught the tow-rope of the *Happy Ted*, and made it fast to his own boat. Then, with a chug-chug-chug, his long canal-boat disappeared into the dark hole of the tunnel, and behind it went the *Happy Ted*.

How dark it was! Ann looked back and saw the hole they had come in by. It looked like a far-off speck of light now. Further into the tunnel they went and further. It grew darker still and the air was musty and damp.

The walls were dripping wet. It was somehow rather frightening and Ann cuddled up to Mummy, pulling her mack round her, for she felt very cold.

Suddenly she looked up and saw another tunnel right above her! She jumped in fright. 'It's all right,' said Mummy, 'that was only an air-hole going right up through the hill to the top and coming out into the open air. We have to have a bit of fresh air here and there in this tunnel, you know!'

There were three or four air-holes and they were strange to look through. Far, far away at the top of them was a speck of light. Ann wished the tunnel would come to an end.

Chug–chug–chug–chug, went the motor of the boat in front, sounding oddly loud in the round dark tunnel. Chug–chug–chug–chug! Water trickled off the walls nearby, and the canal looked deep and black. Nobody spoke at all.

Then Mike gave a cry that made everyone jump. 'Look! What's that? That red thing gleaming in front of us, like a giant's eye!'

'Ah, that's only another boat coming towards us!' said the boatman. 'Now listen, and you'll hear him tooting to tell us to keep to our side of the wall.'

'Too-toot-tootooot!' came the call from the tug coming towards them. And the two canal-boats answered at once. 'Too-too-too-tootoot!' Ann wished she could blow the strange trumpet that the old boatman blew.

Their boat and the tug that was pulling them kept close to their own side of the wall, scraping against it to let the other boat pass. Behind it came two more boats, full of goods. Bump-bump-bump. The boats scraped together now and again, for the tunnel was narrow.

Then they were gone, and the children saw only a faint light in the distance, getting smaller and smaller.

'I wish this tunnel would end,' sighed Ann. 'I don't like it any more. It's too long. I like the locks better.'

'You look out in front of you,' said the boatman, and he pointed ahead. Ann looked – and to her delight she saw a round patch of daylight coming nearer and nearer.

'Hurrah!' said Mike. 'We're getting to the end of it. Soon be out now!'

Cold and wet, the children at last came out into the blazing sunshine, and how they loved the feel of the warm sun on their heads and shoulders! They flung off their damp macks at once.

The power-boat in front threw back their tow-rope to them, called goodbye and went off up the canal, chug-chug-chug-chug!

'There's Clopper waiting for us!' said Mike, pleased. 'I guess he wondered where we had all gone to. Clopper, you did better to go over the hill than through it!'

Once again they went on up the canal, with Clopper pulling well. How peaceful it was! How lovely to have a picnic meal on the deck of the long boat, sitting on the cargo, watching the green banks slip slowly by.

'Where are we going to sleep tonight?' asked Mike. 'We'll never all get into that little cabin!'

'We're going back to the *Saucy Jane*, of course,' said Daddy. 'We can easily catch a bus. We'll be back in no time.'

'In *no* time!' said Belinda, surprised. 'But it has taken us all day to get here – and soon the sun will be going down!'

But Daddy was right. When they said goodbye

to the canal-boat folk, and got on the bus, they were back at the *Saucy Jane* in an hour's time! How extraordinary.

'A canal-boat is a fine peaceful way of getting about,' said Daddy, 'but nobody could call it fast. Well, here we are at the dear old *Saucy Jane*. She looks pretty and peaceful enough, in the setting sun.'

'We've had a lovely, exciting day,' said Mike. 'We may have gone at only about two miles an hour – but we've had time to see even the smallest flower at the edge of the water. Oh, I wish I lived on a canal-boat! I'll buy one when I grow up, and you girls can come with me and live on it. What a time we'll have!'

12

Goodbye to the *Saucy Jane*

The holidays went by too quickly. August slipped away and September came in. Clopper had come back a long while ago and Beauty had gone back to work. All the children could swim like fishes, and each of them could row and steer a boat just as well as Daddy could.

The *Happy Ted* passed them once or twice more, and they always waved and called out their news. They knew other boats, too, and once they had gone off again for the day in another boat – but this time they had gone down the canal instead of up.

'I want to go downhill this time.' Ann had said, so she had her wish. There was a tunnel on the way, but all three children had got out and walked over the hill with the horse. No more long dark tunnels for them! One was enough.

They had learnt many things besides swimming, diving and boating. They had learnt the ways of the wild creatures of the water, and had grown to love the great long-legged herons that sometimes visited the canal, and the white swans who now came to be fed every morning.

They were all brown and strong. Their legs and arms were sturdy with swimming and rowing. Daddy and Mummy were proud of their three children.

'It was the best holiday we could have chosen for them!' said Mummy. 'The very best. They've been good children, helpful and sensible and kind – and what a lot they've learnt.'

It was sad to have to think of leaving the *Saucy Jane*. But now the evenings were getting chilly, and often a low mist came over the water that made the children shiver.

'I don't want to go, though,' said Ann. 'I want to stay all the year round, Mummy.'

'You wouldn't like it, Ann,' said Mummy. 'You are not a child of the canal. You would shiver and get cold and be miserable. It is all right for the summer – but now that the autumn is coming, we must get back to our cosy caravans.'

'And there's school, too,' said Mike. 'I like school. I want to play games again with the other boys and read my books and do carpentering.'

'I like school, too,' said Belinda. They all went to boarding-school, but each weekend they returned to the caravans. And how cosy those caravans were in the wintertime, when the curtains were drawn, the lamps were lighted, and the stove glowed warmly! Games and books and television – yes, winter was good as well as summer.

They cleaned the *Saucy Jane* well. Belinda scrubbed the decks and made them spotless. Ann helped Mummy to turn out all the neat cupboards. Mike and Daddy repainted the little boat that belonged to the *Saucy Jane*.

'Auntie Molly will ask us again if we leave her houseboat better even than we found it!' said Belinda. 'Mummy, do you think she will?'

'I shouldn't be surprised,' said Mummy. 'Well fancy, we have only broken one cup and one plate, and those I have managed to replace. And except for the ink that Mike split on the rug I really don't believe we have done any damage at all.'

'I'll pay for the rug to be cleaned,' said Mike, and Mummy said yes, he could. Once that was done, the boat would be as perfect as when they first came aboard.

They packed their things into the two trunks they had brought with them. They locked up the *Saucy Jane*, and Mike took the key across to Mrs Toms She was sorry to see them go.

'I've got fond of the *Saucy Jane* Family!' she said. 'I'll miss you. Come again next year!'

The car came driving up and everyone got in. Daddy had already gone off with Clopper, riding on his back. Everybody felt a little sad.

'Goodbye, *Saucy Jane*,' said Mike. 'We did love

living in your little cabins, sunning ourselves on your white deck, and feeling you bob up and down on the little waves!'

'Goodbye, swans,' said Ann. 'I'm afraid you won't get bread for your breakfast tomorrow. But I expect Mrs Toms will feed you if you go to her.'

'Goodbye, canal!' said Belinda. 'I've loved every minute of you and all the wild things that belong to you, and the long painted boats that slide over you day by day. Goodbye.'

'Now don't let's get miserable about saying good-bye,' said Mummy. 'We may no longer be the *Saucy Jane* Family, but we shall soon be the Caravan Family again – and we shall say "hallo" to the two caravans, and to dear old Davey and Clopper!'

Off they went in the car. Nobody said a word for a little while, because they were all thinking of the happy *Saucy Jane*. But then they began to think of the caravans.

'I can collect the wood each day for our fire, Mummy,' said Mike.

'I can fetch eggs and butter from the farm,' said Ann.

'I can keep our caravan tidy and clean like I used to,' said Belinda. 'Oh, Mummy – won't it be fun to be back again in our houses on wheels! One for you and Daddy and one for us children! I'm longing to see the caravans again.'

And how lovely they looked when they *did* see

them. There they stood in a pretty field, all newly painted, clean and bright. The children tumbled out of the car with a shout.

'Hallo, caravans! We're back again. Hallo, darling Davey, have you missed us? Clopper and Daddy will soon be back!'

Soon the fire was going and Mummy was cooking their first caravan meal. It was good to be back after all. Daddy was pleased to see such smiling faces when he arrived on Clopper.

'Hallo, Caravan Family!' he said. 'It's a funny thing, but you're JUST as nice as the *Saucy Jane* Family!'

And he was right about that, wasn't he?

The
Pole Star
Family

Contents

1

Granny's Good Idea

Everyone thought that Mike, Belinda and Ann were very lucky children. 'Fancy having a caravan to live in each weekend!' said Kenneth, one of their school friends.

'*Two*,' said Mike. 'Painted red and yellow. One for Mummy and Daddy and one for us three. It's fun.'

'And there are taps in each caravan that really turn on, and bunks for us to sleep in,' said Belinda. 'When the night is warm we have our door open so that we can see right out in the field. It's lovely in buttercup time. The buttercups grow right up to the caravan steps!'

'It does sound lovely,' said Kenneth. 'And didn't you live in a houseboat on the river once?'

'We lived in the *Saucy Jane* on a canal,' said Ann. 'We had a glorious time. Oh, I do wish we could go in a boat again!'

'Yes, but I'd like to go in a boat that travels about,' said Mike. 'Our houseboat stayed still. Wouldn't I like to go in a steamer!'

'What, far away to foreign lands?' said Kenneth.

'You don't mean all by yourself, do you?'

'Oh, *no* – with our whole family,' said Mike. 'We do everything together. It wouldn't be fun, somehow, if we couldn't enjoy things with one another.'

'I think you're a lucky family,' said Kenneth, and all the others agreed. 'Lovely things are always happening to you.'

But oh dear – horrid ones happened too. The very next day, which was Saturday, Mummy had a telegram that said Granny was very ill. She called to Daddy.

'Oh, Daddy – look at this. I must go at once. Can you see to the children this weekend?'

'Yes, of course,' said Daddy, 'and Belinda is very sensible now. We can trust her to do the shopping and a bit of cooking. Can't we, Belinda?'

'Oh yes,' said Belinda, 'but Mummy – poor old Granny! Do take her some flowers from us all, won't you?'

Mummy went off in a hurry, looking worried. The caravan family set to work to tidy up the caravans, and then Belinda went off to do the shopping.

She did hope that Granny wasn't *very* ill. Granny was a darling. She was kind and generous and liked making jokes. She had been going to come and stay with them in the caravans, when Daddy went away for a week, at the end of summer term. Now perhaps she wouldn't.

When the end of term came Granny was still ill. And then, in August, something else happened! Mike began to cough badly, and then he suddenly made a very odd whooping noise.

'Oh dear!' said Mummy. 'That sounds like whooping-cough to me. What a good thing it is the summer holidays, and you won't miss any school. Daddy, as Granny is now in a nursing-home, I think I'd better take him to her house, and hope that Belinda and Ann won't get it. They can stay here in the caravans with you.'

Belinda and Ann were very sad. Poor Mike. All alone at Granny's in the summer holidays. And even Granny wasn't there!

But in a week's time both Belinda and Ann had whooping-cough too, so Mike was brought back to the caravan, and they were once more all together. Mike had it badly and so had Ann, but Belinda whooped only once or twice.

'What a summer holiday,' groaned poor Mummy. 'Granny ill all the time – though she's really getting on now, thank goodness – and now the children down with whooping-cough!'

'We are certainly not a very lucky family at the moment,' said Mike, gloomily, and coughed.

The holidays went by. The summer was not a very good one, and Mummy was quite in despair, because, she said, the children needed a lot of sunshine, and were getting hardly any. They nearly left the caravans and went to stay at Granny's.

Soon the autumn term came near. Mummy looked at her three pale-faced children and felt sad. 'They need a good holiday with plenty of sunshine,' she told Granny, when next she went to see her. 'I don't like sending them back to school looking so pale.'

Granny took her hand. 'Now you listen to me, my dear,' she said. 'I've got a great idea. You know that the doctor says I must go away for a holiday in a ship somewhere – on a cruise. Well, I don't want to go alone. I want you all to come with me. It will do the children such a lot of good – and you too!'

Mummy looked at Granny in astonishment. 'A cruise! Oh, Mother! What an idea – why, we couldn't possibly do such . . .'

'Yes, you could. I shall pay for you all. It would please me so much – and think how the children would love to go off in a great steamer, and see all kinds of different countries!'

'Yes, they would. Oh, they'd *love* it!' said Mummy, beginning to feel most excited. 'I must go back to the caravans and see what their father says. Dear me, what *will* the children say when they hear!'

She kissed Granny goodbye and hurried off, her eyes shining. What a holiday that would be! How

Mike would love it – and as for Belinda and Ann, they would go quite mad with joy. If only, only, only it could really happen!

2

Shall We Go?

Mummy hurried back to the caravans with her news. The children saw her coming and flew to meet her. 'How is Granny? Did you give her the heather we sent her? When is she coming out of the nursing-home?'

'Very soon now,' said Mummy. 'Where's Daddy? I've got some news for him.'

'Good news, or bad?' asked Mike. Belinda looked at him scornfully.

'Can't you see Mummy's face? It's *good* news, of course, isn't it, Mummy? What is it?'

'I can't tell you yet,' said Mummy. 'Ah, there's Daddy.' She ran across the field to the stream, where Daddy was rinsing something.

'It would be nice to have some good luck for a change,' said Mike gloomily. 'We've been a very bad-luck family lately. I hated having whooping-cough.'

'Well, you haven't got it now,' said Ann. 'You've stopped coughing. Or almost. And when you do cough it's only just to remind yourself that you've had it!'

'Don't be silly,' said Mike, and walked off. Mike wasn't quite himself. He was rather bad-tempered and moody. Mummy said it was because he'd had whooping-cough so badly, and wanted a change.

Presently Mummy and Daddy both came over to where the children sat in a row on the steps of their caravan, one above the other. Mummy was smiling.

Ann suddenly felt excited. She jumped up and ran to her mother. 'What is it? You look like Christmas-time, all happy and full of good secrets!'

'I feel like that too,' said Mummy. 'Now listen, children – how would you like to miss school for a few weeks and go holidaying with me and Daddy and Granny?'

'Oooh,' said Ann, thrilled. Mike and Belinda looked at Mummy. They had been rather looking forward to going back to school – somehow these holidays had been too long.

'Where to?' asked Mike cautiously.

'Oh, to Portugal – and Spain – and the Canary Isles – and down to North Africa,' said Mummy, airily.

'But Mummy! Mummy, do you mean it? What, right away across the sea – in a ship?' shouted Mike.

'Yes, in a big steamer,' said Daddy, smiling. 'It's what you've always wanted to do, Mike, isn't it?'

'I can't believe it,' said Mike, looking as if he were about to burst with joy. His face went as red as the poppies in the field.

'Well, you haven't told us if you'd like to go yet,' said Daddy, with a chuckle. The three children threw themselves on him and almost pulled him over.

'Daddy! You know we want to go. It would be too super for words. When are we going? How long for? What is our ship? How . . .'

'Let's all sit down and talk about it,' said Mummy, smiling happily. 'Now listen – the doctor has said that Granny *must* go away on a cruise. . . .'

'What's a cruise?' asked Ann at once.

'A voyage in a ship,' said Mummy. 'Well, Granny doesn't want to go alone, she wants us all to go with her. In the ordinary way you couldn't, because of school – but as you all look so pale and washed-out with that horrid whooping-cough, Daddy and I think it would be a good idea to do as Granny says – and all go off together!'

'Oh, Mummy – it's glorious,' said Belinda. 'Let's make plans at once. Shall we go tomorrow?'

'Dear me, no,' said Mummy. 'There are tickets to get and clothes to pack, the caravans to store somewhere, and the horses to see to.'

'But I can't possibly wait more than a day,' said Ann.

Everyone laughed. That was so like Ann.

'Well, darling, would you like to go off by yourself?' said Mummy. 'I daresay I could arrange it.'

But no – that wouldn't do at all. 'I'll wait,' said Ann, with a sigh. 'I do hope it comes quickly, though.

Oh, fancy – we'll be sleeping on board a big ship, right out to sea! You don't think we shall get shipwrecked, do you, Daddy?' she asked after a moment's thought.

'I shouldn't think so,' said Daddy. 'But there are plenty of lifeboats in case we do, you know. And anyway, we can all swim and float.'

'We're a lucky family again,' said Mike. 'We've been unlucky for weeks – now we're lucky. Shall we start packing this very minute?'

'Darling, we are not going till the beginning of October,' said Mummy. 'Two whole weeks to wait. Granny won't be allowed to go till then. If I were you I'd find an atlas and see exactly where our ship will go. Daddy will tell you.'

So, for the next few hours, Mike, Belinda and Ann studied an atlas harder than they had ever studied one at school!

'We shall start at Southampton – here it is – and go down the Solent, look – and then down south. Here is Portugal – and we'll go round a bit of Spain – and then to Madeira or on to the Canary Isles – what a lovely, lovely name!'

'And then to Africa. Will there be monkeys there?'

'There'll be three extra when *you* arrive!' said Mummy. 'What a lovely time we shall all have!'

3

Off to Southampton at Last!

The next two weeks passed rather slowly, because the children were so impatient, and found it difficult to wait till the day came for setting off. Belinda got the idea that it would be helpful if she and Ann got all their things together to pack.

She found warm jerseys, a thick winter coat for each of them, and even got out their warm vests and knickers. Mummy came to see what she and Ann were doing.

'We've got all our clothes ready for you,' said Belinda, proudly. Mummy stared at the pile of warm jerseys, coats and vests. Then she laughed.

'Darling! We're taking all our summery things! It will be autumn when we leave and come back – but it will be hotter than summer on the trip! We shan't want any of those things; just your thinnest frocks and sunsuits and sandals, that's all.'

'Gracious!' said Belinda. 'I didn't think of that. Oh Mummy, how glorious! Will it really be as hot and sunny as summertime?'

'Hotter,' said Mummy. 'So put all those things away

again, silly. I'm going to take you into the nearest town to buy you all a few more cotton things. And myself too.'

Daddy got the tickets for them all. They were to travel on a big ship called the *Pole Star*. He showed them a picture of her.

'She looks simply beautiful,' said Mike. 'She's all white. Daddy, where will our cabins be? Up on deck?'

'Oh, no,' said Daddy. 'I've got three cabins for us just below water-level; they will be nice and cool.'

'Shan't we have any portholes to look out of?' said Belinda, disappointed. 'I did want to look out of those round holes you see in the side of big ships.'

'Yes, you'll have a porthole!' said Daddy, laughing. 'It will be just above the level of the water – the waves will sometimes splash against it!'

That sounded good. The children gazed at the picture of the big ship. There were two decks, one above the other. There was a high part that Daddy called the bridge.

'That's where the captain stands, at the wheel,' said Daddy.

'Where's the engine-room?' asked Mike. 'I shall want to see the engines make the ship go.'

'Down below the water-level,' said Daddy. 'You shall see everything when we get on board. There will be plenty of time, for there will be days when we don't touch land at all.'

'Oh dear, I wish it would come,' sighed Ann. 'How many more days? Tomorrow, and the day after – and then, THE DAY!'

It came at last, of course. The caravans had been pulled into the town the day before and left in a big garage. Davey and Clopper, the two horses, had been lent to a farmer. Mummy, Daddy and the children all went to spend the last night at Granny's.

Granny was home now, looking a bit thinner, but very cheerful and excited. 'Well!' she said, kissing the children, 'aren't we going to have a lovely holiday together? I hope you've all made up your minds not to fall overboard. It's such a nuisance if the ship has to keep stopping to pick up children from the sea!'

They laughed. 'We won't fall over,' said Mike. 'You forget we lived for quite a long time on a houseboat, Granny. We're used to being careful.'

'When do we start?' said Ann.

'Early tomorrow morning,' said Daddy. 'We go up to London in a car, and catch the train to Southampton. We shall be on board at half-past two. The *Pole Star* is due to leave at four o'clock.'

'Oh, it sounds lovely,' said Ann. 'I shall go to bed almost directly after tea today, to make tomorrow come sooner. Oh, Mummy, you don't think anything will happen to stop us going, do you?'

'I don't see why anything should,' said Mummy. 'Now you eat your tea, Ann. You've had that bit of bread and butter on your plate for ages.'

'I can't eat anything,' said Ann. 'I feel full up with excitement – yes really, Mummy, as if I'd eaten a whole lot of excitement and couldn't eat any more.'

At last THE morning came. Everyone was awake early. All the trunks were ready. The sun shone down brilliantly, and made it real holiday weather. There was a sudden toot-toot in the drive.

'The car, the car! Quick, Daddy, the car!' yelled Mike.

'Well, it won't vanish in thin air if we keep it waiting a moment,' said Daddy. 'Now you take this bag, Mike. Tell the driver to come in and help me.'

And then in a few minutes they were all speeding off to London. Then they were in a big railway station, packed with people – and then in the train to go down to Southampton. They were off to the sea!

Lunch in the train, then a gathering together of bags. The train slid slowly into a big station and stopped.

'Southampton!' yelled Mike, making everybody jump. 'Our ship's here somewhere. Come along, let's go and find it! Hurrah, hurrah!'

4

All Aboard the *Pole Star!*

'We must go to the docks to find our ship, the *Pole Star*,' said Daddy. 'Mike, come back. You won't find it just outside the station, silly boy! It's a long way away.'

So it was. And when they did at last arrive at the docks, the children fell silent in awe. The steamers were so very, very big – much bigger than they had ever imagined!

'Oh, Daddy – why, they're ENORMOUS!' said Mike, almost in a whisper. Their porter smiled at him.

'You look over there, sonny – you'll see the finest ship there is!' he said. 'The *Queen Elizabeth*. She's just in.'

They all stared at the *Queen Elizabeth*. Mike felt a lump coming into his throat. He felt so very proud of that beautiful British ship. There she lay beside the dock, towering high, gleaming with paint, her funnels topping her grandly.

'Oh – I didn't dream we should see *her*,' said Mike at last. 'I never in my life thought I'd see such a big ship. Why, she must take thousands of people!'

'She does,' said the porter. 'She's a floating town.

Grand sight, isn't she? Ah, there's nobody can beat us Britons at ships. Now then – we'll find the *Pole Star*.'

'There she is, there she is!' shouted Belinda, suddenly. 'Just nearby.'

So she was. The children looked at her in delight. She was small compared with the *Queen Elizabeth* – but all the same much, much bigger than they had expected. She was gleaming white from top to toe.

'A beautiful ship too,' said Daddy. 'Fast, comfortable, and with lovely lines. Well, we'll go aboard. Come, Granny, I'll help you up the gangway.'

There was a kind of little wooden bridge stretching down from the *Pole Star's* second deck to the dock where they stood. 'So that's the gangway,' said Belinda. 'I always wanted to go up a proper gangway. Bags I go first!'

Up she went, and Mike and Ann followed. Daddy was helping Granny. A sailor came behind, his hand on Mummy's elbow, for sometimes the ship moved, and the gangway moved with it.

And now at last they were on board ship. Ann gazed up and down the deck. It seemed very long indeed. There were scores of people, carrying bags and packages. Sailors in their dark blue suits went about their business. Ann thought they looked very nice indeed.

'We'll go and find our cabins first, and put our odds and ends there,' said Mummy. A sailor took her down some steps into a big room that looked like a lounge. Then down some more steps still.

'We're going down into the heart of the ship!' said Belinda. 'Gracious, are our cabins right down here?'

They went down a passage lit by electric light, and came to three doors in a row. Numbers 42, 43, 44. The sailor opened the first door.

'Oh!' said Ann, looking in, 'what a lovely place. But look – we've got proper beds to sleep in. I thought we'd have bunks. And there's a wash-basin too. And a little dressing-table with drawers – and even a wardrobe! Goodness, it's like a proper bedroom.'

'It's got a porthole!' cried Mike, in delight, and ran to it. 'Oh, look – the water's just below it. Do look! Can we open it, sailor?'

'If you like,' said the man, smiling. 'As long as we're in calm water, it's all right. Shut it when we leave, or you'll get a wave splashing on to the bed!'

It was strange, looking out of the round window. The glass was very, very thick, not a bit like ordinary window glass. No wave could possibly break it. The children could hear the water lapping outside. It was a lovely sound.

'Put all your things down for a while,' said Mummy. 'We must go up on deck. You'll want to be there when we move off, won't you?'

They left the cabin. They peeped into numbers 43 and 44, which were just exactly the same. There were two beds in each. Mummy and Granny were to share a cabin, and Mike and Daddy, and Belinda and Ann. Mike felt very grown-up to be sharing with Daddy. What fun it would be to go to bed in a cabin just below water-level!

They all went up on deck. What a noise and bustle there was! Steamers were blowing their sirens, gulls were screaming, sailors were shouting, and there was a terrific noise of creaking and winding, as all kinds of luggage was hauled up by a crane and dropped into the hold.

The children found a place by the deck-rail and looked over. People were still streaming up the gangway. The crane placed a great pile of luggage in the hold and then swung itself out over the dock-side again to pick up the last lot.

An enormous noise made the children almost jump out of their skins. 'It's all right,' said Daddy, amused, 'that's our own ship's voice – her siren. It's to warn everyone that we're going soon. Look, they are going to pull in the gangway so that nobody else can board us.'

Then the children noticed a rumbling noise that seemed to come from the heart of the ship – the engines were starting. They would soon be off!

'We're moving, we're moving!' shouted Mike, suddenly, in excitement. 'Look, the dock-side is going away from us. We're off, we're off!'

Everyone shouted and waved. 'Goodbye, goodbye!' The children yelled too. 'Goodbye. We're really off! We're really OFF!'

5

Goodbye, England!

The great ship moved slowly along the dock towards the open sea. Mike saw some little tugs that appeared to be joined to her by ropes. Could they be pulling her?

'Oh, yes – they're guiding her out and helping her,' said Daddy. 'Look, there's the sea. Now look back at the docks and see the masses of ships there, of all kinds – some unloading cargoes, some taking in goods, some waiting for passengers, some wanting coal and water, others waiting for repairs.'

'It's all wonderful,' said Mike, who looked happier than he had ever been in his life. 'All those ships and steamers and cranes. To think that the ships have been all over the world and back many, many times. Oh, I wish I was a sailor. Daddy, can I be one when I grow up?'

'If you badly want to,' said Daddy. 'You must wait and see. You wanted to be a bus-driver the other day. You might change your mind again.'

'I shan't, I shan't,' said Mike. 'I want to be a sailor with a ship of my very own. I shall call it the *Belinda Ann*.'

'Very nice too,' said Daddy. 'Now look – here we are out on the open sea. You'll feel the swell of the waves in a moment.'

'Oh, yes!' said Belinda. 'The ship isn't only moving forwards – she's moving a bit from side to side – rolling a little. I like it. She's come alive!'

'Yes, she's come alive,' said Mike. 'I say, I hope we get a storm. How grand to feel the *Pole Star* riding enormous waves, going up and down, and from side to side!'

'Well, I hope we don't,' said Granny. 'I shouldn't like that at all. I should probably be very seasick.'

'We're none of us going to be seasick,' said Mike. 'We've made up our minds not to be. We don't want to waste a single minute of this trip in being seasick.'

'Now the little tugs have gone,' said Ann. 'Good-bye, little tugs. I liked you. You were such busy, clever little things, fussing around.'

'I'm hungry,' said Mike. 'And yet I don't feel as if I can possibly leave my place to have tea.'

'Well, you must,' said Mummy, firmly. 'Come along. We'll go down to the dining-room and have tea. I'm sure Granny is dying for some!'

They went down the stairs to the second deck, and then down steps to the lounge. A steward brought them a lovely tea, with plenty of little cakes.

'Do we have nice food on board ship?' asked Belinda.

'Very nice,' said Daddy. 'Ann, do eat. Or are you still full up with excitement?'

'I am rather,' said Ann, with a huge sigh. 'But these cakes do look so nice. I really must have some. Oh, Granny, do you like our ship?'

'I love it,' said Granny. 'Wasn't it a good idea of mine?'

'The best idea you ever had in your life, Granny,' said Belinda. 'Mummy, what can we do when we've finished? May we go on deck again? On the top deck of all? I want to see the land we pass.'

'Yes, if you like,' said Mummy. 'I need not tell any of you to be careful, not to play any silly tricks on board ship, and to come back to us every now and again so that we know you're all right.'

'I'll look after the girls, Mummy,' said Mike. 'Daddy, are we going down the Solent? Shall we soon see the last of England?'

'Yes,' said Daddy. 'The very last. Go on up now if you want to. We'll come later.'

The *Pole Star* was now well out to sea. Southampton had been left far behind. The children could see the Isle of Wight on one side and the mainland on the other. The *Pole Star* seemed to them to be going quite fast.

'See that long white tail behind her?' said Mike. 'That's called the wake. It's the sea-water all churned up till it's white.'

'We've still got gulls all round us,' said Belinda. 'I like them. I like the funny mewing noise they make too.'

'It sounds as if they were laughing sometimes,' said Mike. 'Oh, look – is that the end of the Isle of Wight? We're going quite near it.'

Dusk was now beginning to come over the sea. Lights sprang up on the big ship. Little lights twinkled here and there from other boats in the distance. Mummy came up behind the children.

'It's goodbye to England now,' she said. 'We're going swiftly away from her. Tomorrow we shall be in the Bay of Biscay, and it may be very rough. I hope not, though.'

'I shan't mind!' said Mike. 'Are we going to France?'

'No. Our first stop is at Lisbon, in Portugal,' said Mummy. 'Now, if you want to stop up here you must put coats on. It's a bit chilly tonight – though very soon we shall feel so hot that we shall want to take our clothes off and bathe all day long!'

'What I want to do,' said Ann, 'is to go to bed in one of those cabins. Oh, Mummy – fancy going to bed under the water, and hearing the waves lapping against the side of the ship. Do you know, I really think I'll go now!'

6

Bedtime on Board Ship

Excitement had made Granny tired too. She said that she didn't think she would stay up to dinner that night. She would go to her cabin and have it there.

'May *we* stay up to dinner?' said Mike, excited at the thought of being with the grown-up people in the big dining-room each night.

'Certainly not,' said Mummy. 'You can't do that till you're much older. You can have a nice supper in your cabin. The cabin steward will bring it to you. I'll choose something good and have it sent down.'

'What about baths?' said Belinda. 'Do we have baths on board ship?'

'Of course!' said Mummy. 'There is a bathroom at the end of our little passage, just for us six to use. You must have a bath every night, just as you do at home. You can have your supper in the girls' cabin with them each night, Mike, if you like, and go along to your own afterwards.'

It all sounded very thrilling. They went to find the bathroom. It was very tiny, but very nice. The bath was green and had huge shining taps. The water came out scalding hot. There were thick green towels too, marked P.S.

'P.S. How funny – that's what you put at the end of a letter, isn't it, if you want to add a bit more,' said Belinda.

'P.S. stands for *Pole Star*, silly,' said Mike. 'I say, I wonder if the bath-water runs away into the sea.'

'Of course it does,' said Belinda. 'Goodness, the ship rolled quite a bit then. I almost fell into the bath.'

'Yes, you'll have to get your sea-legs,' said Daddy, putting his head into the bathroom. 'If she rolls much more you must be careful to hang on to the hand-rails.'

They each had a bath in turn. Then Ann brushed Belinda's hair a hundred times and Belinda brushed Ann's. Mummy always made them brush their hair one hundred times. She said that made it shine brightly.

They cleaned their teeth at the little basin, and then the steward arrived with their supper.

'Ooooh!' said Ann, looking at the trays. 'What a wonderful supper. Thank you very much.'

'Grapefruit with cherries on top!' said Mike.

'A cup of the most delicious-smelling soup in the world,' said Belinda. 'And look at these little squares of toast.'

'And a pink jelly,' said Ann. 'My favourite. Oh, jelly, are you cold? You do shiver so. Never mind, you'll soon be warm inside me!'

Everyone laughed. They sat on the beds to eat their supper. They were very happy. It was all so new and strange and lovely. And it was only just beginning!

'The nicest part of a holiday is the beginning,' said Mike. The ship gave a roll as he said that, and his jelly ran off the plate. 'Oh, goodness – look at my jelly! It's on your bed, Ann.'

'Well, spoon it off then,' said Ann. 'I say, I hope we don't roll off our beds at night.'

'We might if it was very, very rough,' said Mike, spooning up the jelly. 'The beds are clamped to the floor, look – *they* won't move.'

Ann climbed up on to her bed and looked out of the porthole window. It was tight shut now, and the children had been told that they were not to try and open it till they were in port again. She could see nothing through it at all, except darkness.

'Do you suppose we say our prayers on board ship?' she said, slipping down to the bed again.

'Why ever not?' said Mike, astonished. 'What difference does it make where we are?'

'Well – it will seem a bit odd to kneel down on a floor that keeps moving about,' said Ann. 'I shall have to hold on to my bed.'

'I've got a lot of prayers to say tonight,' said Belinda. 'I shall say thank you for this lovely holiday, and ask for all of us to be kept safe, and for there to be no shipwreck, and for Davey and Clopper to be happy while we're away, and . . .'

'Well, let's all be quiet and say them at the same time,' said Mike. So for a few minutes there was no sound in the little cabin except for the waves slapping against the side of the ship. Then Ann scrambled into her bed and Belinda into hers. They were soft and springy, and the two girls cuddled down into them with delight.

Granny came in to say goodnight. She was in her dressing-gown ready to get into bed too. 'Did you have the same supper as we did?' asked Ann. 'Oh Granny, isn't it *fun* to be on board ship? I'm longing to wake up tomorrow morning and remember where I am!'

Then Mummy and Daddy came in. They had dressed for dinner and looked very grand. 'You're beautiful, Mummy,' said Belinda, hugging her. 'Goodnight! I don't want to go to sleep for ages, but I'm afraid I shall go at once. My eyes keep shutting.'

Mike went off to his cabin. Mummy had told him he could read for half an hour, as he was older than the girls. But he didn't want to. He just wanted to lie in his little bed and feel the movement of the ship. To and fro, to and for, and then a little bit forward and backward.

'It's lovely,' said Mike to himself. 'I shall be a sailor when I grow up. I shall be the captain of a ship like this. I shall . . .'

But by that time he was asleep – and in his dreams he was captain of the *Pole Star*. What a wonderful dream!

7

Land Ahoy!

It was lovely waking up next morning, and
remembering everything. Ann sat up and reached
over to Belinda's bed. She gave her sister a poke.

'Belinda! We're on the sea! Do wake up.'

Then Mike came in, beaming. 'Are you awake?
It's a gorgeous morning. I've been up on deck in my
dressing-gown, and the sea's lovely. Do get up.'

They got up and washed and dressed. They went
on deck, and felt the sun pouring down on them. The
sky was blue and the sea was blue-purple. Everything
was glorious.

There was no land to be seen at all. It was an
extraordinary feeling to stand there by the deck-rail,
and see nothing but water round them, stretching for
miles and miles. There was not even another ship to
be seen.

'If this is the Bay of Biscay it's jolly calm,' said
Mike, half-disappointed. 'I say – let's explore the
ship, shall we?'

'After breakfast,' said Mummy, coming up behind
them. 'Come along, there's a lovely breakfast waiting

for you – six different kinds of cereal to choose from, more grapefruits if you want them, and about twelve different dishes to choose from: bacon and eggs, ham, fish . . .'

'I certainly *shall* be a sailor when I grow up!' said Mike. 'You make me feel awfully hungry, Mummy.'

They explored the ship from top to toe after breakfast. They ran down both the upper and lower decks. There were countless deck-chairs there, and many people were sitting in them reading or snoozing in the sun.

The children found a swimming-pool at one end of the ship and were delighted. 'Fancy a swimming-pool on a ship! We can bathe every day!' said Mike.

They found a nice sun-deck too, just under the captain's bridge. Mummy thought it would be lovely to sit there with Granny.

'There's everything you can possibly want on this ship,' said Mike to his mother. 'Games to play on deck, places to sit, a swimming-pool, places to eat, a reading-room, that big dining-room where we have our meals, a ballroom for dancing . . . Oh, Mummy, there's everything!'

'May we bathe?' asked Belinda. 'In that lovely pool, Mummy?'

'Yes, if you like,' said Mummy, and the three went off to change. What fun they had swimming and diving and going down the chute! Ann wouldn't go down at first, but she did at last, and loved it. Splash! She flew down into the water and gasped.

'This is a lovely holiday,' said Mike. 'I love the *Pole Star*. She's a jolly good ship.'

The children swam, and played deck tennis, throwing the rubber ring over the net to one another; they went down into the engine room to see the engines, and came back hot and dirty.

And then suddenly Belinda noticed something. 'Look!' she said in surprise, 'all the sailors have changed out of their dark-blue suits into white ones! Oh, how nice they look!'

So they had. Daddy laughed at the children's astonished faces. 'Oh, that shows we're leaving the cold weather behind and coming into hot days. You'll have to change into your coolest things soon too.'

One afternoon, when they were all sitting on the sun-deck, something made them jump suddenly. The ship's siren was near the deck, and it suddenly blew a loud, mournful note. 'OOOOOOOOOOOOOOO!'

'It's like a giant cow mooing,' said Ann. 'Oh Daddy – whatever did it do that for?'

'Look out to sea,' said Daddy. 'There's a thick sea-mist coming up. We'll soon be in it. What a pity! We shall soon be coming into Lisbon, and I would have liked you to see Portugal coming nearer.'

But the sea-fog thickened, and the siren hooted continually. Nothing could be seen from the deck.

The sea-mist made it chilly, and the children went down below to play games.

'Is it dangerous?' asked Ann, thinking of ships moving blindly in the fog. 'Shall we bump into something?'

'The captain is up on the bridge, at the wheel,' said Daddy. 'He won't leave it until the fog has cleared and he has brought the ship to safety. He'll be up there for twenty-four hours on end, if need be.'

But when at last the ship steamed into the beautiful harbour at Lisbon, the fog had cleared. Night had come, and the harbour gleamed with lights. The big ship moved to her place in the dock.

'We're staying here for the night,' said Mummy, looking over the deck-rail at all the ships in the harbour, each with its lights showing brightly. 'You'll quite miss the roll of the ship, won't you! Tomorrow we will take you to see the royal palace of Pena, set on the top of a steep rugged hill.'

'Oh – a palace! Did kings live there?' asked Ann. 'Oh Mummy, do you know, it will be quite exciting to walk on land again. I've forgotten what it feels like!'

When the children went to bed that night they opened the porthole of their cabin and gazed out into the quiet harbour. Many big ships were there, and many little fishing-boats too, with red sails. It was lovely to look at them all, rocking a little on the dark water, where all the lights were reflected.

'It even smells different here,' said Ann, sniffing. 'It smells foreign! Oh I say – fancy going to see a palace tomorrow. I'm sure it won't be as grand as our Windsor Castle, though!'

8

Going Ashore

The harbour was even lovelier in the morning, when many boats were moving out. The children liked the bright-sailed fishing-boats most of all. They were quite sorry when Mummy came to say that Daddy was ready to take them to the royal palace at Sintra.

Off they went in a taxi that went much faster than any English one. In about three-quarters of an hour's time they came to a very steep, rugged hill, with a winding road that went up and up to the top.

And there, on the summit, was the palace. 'It *does* remind me just a bit of Windsor Castle,' said Mike. 'Isn't it lovely? Can we go in?'

It was strange to wander through a palace that had once belonged to many long-ago kings. After a while Ann began to worry about the ship.

'Mummy, we'd better go back! Suppose it went without us. Do let's go.'

They went at last, and tore down the hill at breakneck speed in the taxi. Belinda shut her eyes in terror and hoped they would soon be at the bottom.

'Are those palm trees?' asked Mike, as they sped

through the beautiful countryside. 'And what are those mournful-looking trees? Oh, cypresses. And look, I'm sure those are orange trees. And what's that big grove of trees with great green leaves? I've never seen trees like that before.'

'Olive trees,' said Daddy. 'You've heard of olives and olive-oil, haven't you?'

'I'm quite longing to be on board ship again,' said Ann. 'I do hope she hasn't gone without us.'

She hadn't, of course. There she lay in the harbour, gleaming in welcome. They ran up the gangway, feeling as if they had come back home!

'We go to Spain next,' said Granny, welcoming them. She had not been to the palace, because she was still feeling tired. 'To Seville. I know a place there called the House of a Thousand Shawls. Daddy, would you like to go there and choose one for Mummy?'

'I certainly would,' said Daddy. 'And I should like to go to the wonderful cathedral there – yes, and see a bull-ring, though I don't want to see a bull-fight.'

'Oh *no*,' said Mike. 'The poor horses! They haven't any chance against the bulls at all. I should like to see the bull-fighters, though; they must look very grand, and be very brave men.'

The ship sailed on to Spain. It went up a wide river to the old town of Seville.

'Do the Seville oranges you make marmalade of come from this district?' asked Belinda.

'They do,' said Mummy. 'Oh, look at the bulls in those fields, Mike. What big creatures they are!'

Seville was a beautiful town, and the most beautiful thing in it was the cathedral. All the children crept in quietly, awed by its grandeur and beauty. They gazed at the great stained- glass windows.

The sunshine seemed very bright indeed when they came out again. Belinda blinked. 'You know,' she said, 'ordinary little churches are just houses for God – but a cathedral is a palace for Him.'

'And now,' said Granny, 'we'll go to the House of a Thousand Shawls. Come along.'

They went to it. It was a great shop, full of nothing but magnificent shawls. They were spread everywhere, and hung down from the roof and over the walls. Oh, the colours – red and green and blue and orange and black, all embroidered most beautifully.

'Which one will you have?' Daddy asked Mummy. 'What about this deep red one? That would suit you beautifully.'

'Oh yes, have that one, Mummy,' said Belinda. 'I do like the great dark roses embroidered all over it. Isn't Seville a beautiful place, with beautiful things!'

But the bull-ring wasn't so beautiful. They all went to have a look at one. It was quite empty, and was strewn with sawdust. Ann didn't like the smell.

'Let's come away,' she said, pulling at her father's hand. 'I don't like to think of the bulls hurting the horses, and the bull-fighters hurting the bulls, and everyone cheering. Let's go back to the ship with your lovely shawl, Mummy.'

So back they went again, wandering through the Spanish streets, stared at by black-eyed, black-haired girls, who wore little black shawls over their heads. Nobody wore a hat, and they all looked happy and lively, and talked very fast to one another. The children wished they could understand what they said.

Mummy bought each of the girls a tiny gold Spanish bracelet. Mike chose a wooden carving of a bull. They took them proudly back to the *Pole Star*.

'She's hooting, she's hooting,' said Ann, in alarm, as they drew near. 'She's telling us to hurry up!'

'It's all right. There's still half an hour,' said Daddy, laughing. 'Got your shawl, Mummy? Up the gangway, all of you!'

'Now we're off to Madeira, and the Canary Isles,' said Granny. 'We shan't see land for a while. But maybe we shall see a few interesting things – flying-fish, for instance!'

'Flying-fish!' cried Belinda. 'Oh, are there *really* such creatures! I thought they were like unicorns, and only belonged to fairy tales.'

'I'm going to stand at the deck-rail all day tomorrow and look for them!' said Ann. 'Oh Mummy – do you think I could catch one and take it home with me? I *would* like it to fly round the caravan!'

9

Flying-fish, Dolphins – and Bullocks!

The next day the children asked one of the sailors if there was any chance of seeing flying-fish on the trip.

'Oh yes!' said the sailor. 'You watch out, the next day or two. We often see them when we go down south.'

But it was not until two days later that Belinda heard someone shouting loudly. 'Look – flying-fish! Look!'

All the children rushed to the deck-side. Then they saw a strange sight. Rising right out of the sea was a small shoal of gleaming fish! They flew through the air for about half a minute, spreading their great front fins.

They went very fast indeed, and then dived back gracefully into the sea. But in another moment out they flew again, glittering in the sunshine.

'Oh, aren't they lovely!' cried Ann. 'I never, never thought I'd see fish flying. Daddy, how do they fly?'

'Well, they haven't any wings, of course,' said Daddy. 'They swim tremendously fast under water, and then, to escape an enemy, they fling themselves above the surface, and use their long fins to help them.'

'Is there an enemy making them fly now?' asked Mike. 'Oh yes, look – what are those things showing here and there in the water, chasing the flying-fish?'

'Dolphins,' said Daddy. 'See, there they go, leaping right out of the water, a mile a minute! They belong to the whale family. There are few creatures that swim faster than a dolphin!'

The children watched the curious dolphins, with their long, beak-shaped mouths, leaping along after the flying-fish. It was really most exciting. 'I *think* the flying-fish got away,' said Ann, at last. 'Dolphins and flying-fish – I never in my life thought I'd see those.'

The sun grew hotter and hotter as they went more and more south. The children wore as little as they could. The passengers became one big family, for now that there was no land to be seen they had to find their interests on board, and talk and play with one another.

There was lifeboat practice. That was fun. Everyone had to learn where he or she was to go in case of danger. The children knew exactly which lifeboat they were to make for, and how to put on a life jacket quickly, so that if danger came to the *Pole Star* at any time, they would be saved.

'If everyone knows what to do and where to go to, there is no panic or muddle,' Daddy said. 'And we have to remember that, just like whooping-cough, fear is catching, and we must always be brave, especially when we are with a lot of people in danger.'

'Is bravery catching too?' said Mike.

'Oh yes,' said Daddy, 'and it's a very good thing to catch. You want to give it to as many people as you can!'

The days began to slip by too quickly. The sun shone down all the time. And then they came to their next port of call!

'We shall come to the island of Madeira soon,' said Mummy. 'You'll like that. We'll take you for a ride in a bullock cart, down very steep, narrow little streets, lined with small cobble-stones!'

'A *bullock*-cart!' said Belinda. 'I shall like that. Why don't we have bullock-carts at home? I think they would be much nicer than buses.'

Madeira was lovely. The *Pole Star* came nearer and nearer to the sun-drenched island, and at last sailed into harbour there, while many jabbering people ran about ashore, excited and welcoming.

The children were eager to go on shore. It seemed such a long time since they had seen land! They felt peculiar when they walked on the dock. 'The earth seems so solid somehow, after the swing and sway of the ship,' said Mike. 'I've got sea-legs now instead of land-legs!'

Bullock-carts were waiting to take the travellers

for trips. What fun it was to ride in one!

'Why, they have no wheels!' cried Ann, in surprise. 'Look – they have runners, like sledges, instead of wheels Can we get in?'

Some of the streets were very steep indeed, and the cobble-stones bright and slippery. The runners of the bullock-cart slid easily and quickly over them. The big, sleepy-eyed bullocks were strong, and pulled them swiftly along. The children were full of delight.

'Oh Mummy! I wish we had bullock-carts at home, I really do. Oh, why are we stopping?'

'Mummy wants to buy some handmade cloths, said Daddy. 'Look, we'll go into this little shop. You can each choose six handkerchiefs, embroidered by the people of this island – perhaps sewn by children as young as you, Ann.'

It was fun shopping in the unusual little hut. They bought a lot of things and then stepped back into their bullock-cart.

'To the ship, bullocks, please!' said Mike grandly, and down the cobbled street at top speed went the bullocks. Ann gasped. What a pace!

'It's funny to think they may be having cold, rainy weather in England now,' said Mike, fanning himself. 'Look at all those brilliant flowers out – just like summer. And I never felt the sun so hot before. I'm sure I should get sunstroke if I took my hat off!'

'You certainly would,' said Daddy. 'So don't try it.

Now, here we are, back on board again. Where do you think we go to next – to the Canary Isles!'

'Do canaries live there?' asked Ann.

'Of course!' said Daddy. 'You'll see them flying all round you, as common as sparrows!'

'Flying-fish, dolphins, bullocks, canaries,' said Belinda. 'Whatever next!'

10

Everything is so Exciting!

On went their good ship, the *Pole Star*, on and on over the southern seas. And when they came to the Canary Isles, it was just as Daddy had said – there were plenty of wild canaries flying about, and singing loudly!

'But they're not bright yellow like ours at home,' said Mike, disappointed. 'They're green. Still, they sing just as beautifully. Daddy, are there any Parrot Isles? I hope we shall go to them too. I'd like to take home a parrot and teach it to talk.'

'Three parrots in one family are quite enough,' said Mummy. 'Oh, look at those little boys swimming round the ship. They're like fish, they're so much at home in the water.'

Some of the passengers threw pennies into the clear water. A horde of small boys at once dived for them. They did not miss a single penny. It was marvellous to watch them.

'We'll do that in the swimming-pool,' said Mike. 'We'll practise it. It looks quite easy, but I suppose you have to keep your eyes open under water.'

A boy yelled something from the water below. One of the sailors told the passengers what he had said.

'He says, for a shilling he will swim right under the ship and come up the other side,' said the sailor.

'I'll give him a shilling then,' said one of the passengers, and threw one into the water. It circled downwards. The boy swam after it and caught it. He came up to the surface, and waved his hand to everyone at the deckside.

Then down he went and down, at the side of the ship. Soon he was lost to sight. The passengers left that side of the ship and went to the other side to watch the boy coming up there.

Ann was rather scared. 'He can't swim under the ship – it's a long long way down, into the very deep water, where it's dark,' she said. 'Oh Daddy – he won't get caught under the ship, will he? He'll come up, won't he?'

'Of course,' said Daddy. 'He does it a dozen times a day! Now, stand by me and watch for him to come up.'

All the same, it seemed a long time before a little dark speck appeared far down in the water. And then the boy shot up to the surface, gasping, and waved his hand merrily. He had done it!

'Bravo!' shouted the passengers. 'Well, well – right under the ship! How did he have the breath?'

Little boats came out and surrounded the ship,

selling fruit of all kinds – bananas, peaches, oranges, even pineapples. The dark-faced, bright-eyed people shouted their wares, and even climbed up the side of the ship with them.

It was all very exciting. The three children, burnt brown now by the hot sun, enjoyed every new and strange thing they saw. There seemed no end to them. When they went ashore, they found that many of the wild canaries had been caught and put into cages for people to buy.

'Few of them will live to reach England,' said Daddy. 'They are so used to this hot climate, poor little things.'

All the same, many people bought them in little wicker cages. They gave them to the sailors on board ship to keep for them, and the children went to see them every day. They sang their hearts out in the little wicker cages, and Ann longed to set them all free.

'They've not been born and brought up in cages as our cage-canaries have,' she said to Belinda, sadly. 'I'm sure they are unhappy.'

The sailors had put up a rope-line in their quarters, and had hung the little cages all along it. It was an unusual sight to see. The children went along each day to make sure that the birds had water to drink.

The good ship went on again over the bright blue sea. The days seemed to run into one another. The only day the children really knew was Sunday. Then there was a service held on the deck, and all the sailors came too.

The captain read from the Bible, and led the prayers. The children stood there in the sun and the breeze listening. They liked it very much.

'I've never been to church on board a big ship before,' said Ann. 'Mummy, didn't the hymns sound nice sung to the sound of the sea and the wind?'

'Tomorrow will be Monday because this is Sunday,' said Mike. 'I don't know the days any more! By the time tomorrow comes I shall have forgotten it's Monday. That's the extraordinary part about a holiday. You just don't know which day is which – they're all so nice.'

'Where are we going next?' asked Ann.

'To Africa!' said Mummy. 'To French Morocco. And then, my dear – home!'

'Oh, dear – shall we go home so soon?' said Ann, in dismay. 'Can't we go right round the world, Mummy?'

'Good gracious, no,' said Mummy.

'I'll take you and Belinda all round the world when I'm a sailor,' promised Mike. 'We'll stop at any port we like for as long as we want to.'

'There's no land to be seen anywhere now,' said Belinda, looking over the sea. 'Just blue water. Let's go and have a game of deck-tennis. I'll take you on, Mike. Then we'll have a bathe in the swimming-pool. Daddy, will you come and throw pennies for us, please? We're going to be diving-boys!'

'Right,' said Daddy. 'Who'll swim under the ship for a shilling?' But nobody would!

11

A Different Kind of Shopping

The *Pole Star* went on to North Africa. The children stood at the deck-rail and watched the land gradually coming nearer and nearer. They saw a big city spreading before them, a city of gleaming white buildings and wide streets.

'This is Casablanca,' said Daddy. 'If you are good I'll take you ashore and let you go shopping in the bazaars – little streets of native shops where you can buy almost anything!'

'We'll buy presents to take home,' said Mummy. 'We won't go to any of the big shops in the wide streets. We'll go, as Daddy says, to the little native ones.'

So, feeling very thrilled, the three children stepped ashore at Casablanca, their money in their purses.

A taxi took them to the streets of little shops. But almost at once Ann turned to her mother in disgust. 'Mummy! There's the most awful smell. I can't bear it.'

'Oh, there's always an awful smell in these places,' said Mummy. 'Look, here is my bottle of smelling-salts. Hold it to your nose.'

Poor Ann was nearly sick with the smell of the dirty streets. The others put their handkerchiefs over their noses. They looked with interest at the unusual little shops. They sold all kinds of things — hand-made brooches, rings and bracelets, beautiful pottery, slippers with turned-up toes, bags, baskets, brass pots . . .

'They're all quite cheap,' said Daddy. 'But you have to bargain for them.'

'What's bargain?' asked Ann, still sniffing Mummy's smelling-salts.

'Well, I say a low price, and the shopkeeper says a high price, and he comes down a bit, and I go up a bit, and in the end I pay about half what he asks,' said Daddy.

'But why don't they put a proper price on, like we do at home?' asked Belinda. 'It seems such a waste of time.'

'Ah, but they enjoy their bargaining,' said Daddy. 'And they have plenty of time to waste. Now, watch me!'

Daddy wanted to buy some lovely dishes, patterned in all colours. He asked their price, but he spoke in French, because everyone spoke in French in Casablanca.

Then the man said a price and Daddy looked shocked. Daddy said a price, and the man looked horrified. So it went on, and the children laughed to see Daddy and the shopkeeper arguing and haggling vigorously.

At last Daddy paid over some French money and the man gave him the dishes, all smiles. The bargaining was over. The man had got the price he wanted, and Daddy had paid the price he meant to pay, so both were pleased.

'Can I do some bargaining too?' asked Ann. She badly wanted a tiny brooch shaped like a flying-fish.

'Of course you can't, silly,' said Mike. 'You can't talk French.'

'No – I can't,' said Ann. 'Well, I'm going to learn it as fast as I can when I get back to school. I can see it would be very useful. Daddy, please bargain for that flying-fish brooch.'

So Daddy bargained again and got the brooch. Ann was delighted. Then Belinda got a pair of slippers in red, with silver-edged turn-up toes, and Mike got a curious brass pot, carved with little ships.

'I like the lovely things they sell, but oh, how very dirty everything is,' said Ann. 'Look at that meat – and those sweets – all crawling with flies! Why don't the people clean?'

'Perhaps because they haven't been taught to!' said Mike. 'Well, we often grumble at having to wash our hands and put on clean clothes, but I'd rather do that too often than not enough. I shan't grumble about having to clean any more, now I see what happens when people don't.'

'Mummy, stop! Look at this darling little baby,' said Belinda, suddenly. 'But oh, Mummy, it's got flies crawling all round its poor eyes!'

'Poor little thing,' said Mummy, trying to brush them away. But they came back again at once. 'I'm afraid a good many babies go blind because of these dreadful flies. Oh dear, such a beautiful city, and such lovely things in it – but at the back of it all, so much poverty and so many horrid sights.'

'I didn't know before how lucky we are to be born in Britain,' said Mike. 'Why, we might have been born one of these poor little babies, in all this dirt and smelliness!'

'I think I'm going to be sick,' said Ann. 'I want to go back. It smells so bad. I don't want to come here again, not even to buy these lovely things.'

They went back to the ship. Daddy looked at Ann. 'Poor Ann! Well, I wanted you to see how some people have to live. Now, cheer up – I'll take you for a ride over the countryside in a motor-coach, and you can look out for monkeys!'

So off they went that afternoon, and to Ann's joy they saw hundreds and hundreds of monkeys, chattering gaily, swinging from tree to tree. Then they came to a white-walled house, set by the water, and there they drank mint-tea from little cups without any handles.

'Mint-tea!' said Belinda, sniffing it in delight. 'Mummy, can you make some when we go home? It's *much* nicer than ordinary tea.'

'Smells, and monkeys, and mint-tea,' said Ann solemnly. 'We never know what we're going to have any day now!'

12

There's No Place Like Home!

And now the trip would soon be over. The *Pole Star* turned northwards, and left the great white city of Casablanca behind. The next land the children would see would be England!

They began to long for their own country.

'Going to other countries only seems to make our own all the nicer, somehow,' said Belinda. 'I feel as if I really *loved* England now. I keep thinking of things like primroses, and rainy days in April when the sun shines out suddenly, and buttercups all shining gold.'

'So do I,' said Mike. 'We've had a most glorious time, and I'll never forget it, but it's England for me every time! All the same – I shall certainly be a sailor when I grow up. I must see more of the world!'

'There's only one thing we didn't have,' said Ann, 'and that's a storm.'

'Well, there's time for that, Missy,' said a big sailor nearby. 'We're running into one tonight! I can feel it coming. I'll be changing out of my white things into my warm blue ones before many hours are gone!'

'Oooh,' said Ann, her eyes round, 'a storm at sea!

Do you really mean it? Will it be dangerous? Shall we have to take to the lifeboats? What a good thing the *Pole Star* has so many.'

'We won't need the lifeboats this trip,' said the sailor, laughing. 'But you may feel a bit seasick – and don't you come up on deck when the ship starts rolling about!'

The sailor was right. The storm came that night, when the children were in bed in their cabins. The wind began to howl dismally, and big waves blew up. The *Pole Star* began to roll tremendously.

Ann felt a bit scared. 'I don't mind so much when the ship rolls from side to side,' she said to Mummy. 'But I don't like it when it goes up and down the other way. It gives me a funny feeling. I think I might be seasick.'

'Granny's feeling a bit funny too,' said Mummy, smiling. 'A lot of people will get a touch of seasickness if this goes on. But you lie down and suck these barley sugars, and you won't feel so bad.'

The storm went on all night long. Ann screamed when something began to slide about the floor. Belinda put the light on. 'Something's sliding over the floor,' wept Ann. 'What is it, what is it?'

'Oh Ann – it's only that suitcase under your bed,' said Belinda, with a giggle. 'Look, there it comes from under your bed – and now it's gone under mine – and when the ship rolls the other way, it'll come out again and go to yours. Yes, there it is. It'll go to and fro all the time.'

Ann gave a giggle through her tears. It was funny to think of the case popping backwards and forwards like that.

Next morning the sea was still very rough, and the children found it difficult to walk, and very difficult indeed to climb up the stairs. They hung on to the hand-rails and tried to keep their balance as best they could.

'Everything will slide off the breakfast table,' said Mike, but it didn't, because the stewards had put up wooden edges called 'fiddles' at every table, and these stopped the dishes and plates from sliding off.

It was quite a puzzle to eat and drink without spilling anything, when the boat was rolling so much. The children laughed to see people doing their best to stop their plates from rushing away from them.

Daddy took them up on deck to see the angry waters. What enormous waves reared up their grey-green heads! How they slapped against the ship! Some broke on deck and water ran everywhere. It was very thrilling indeed.

But by the time the *Pole Star* was due back in England the storm had gone, the sea was calm, and the October sun shone down serenely. The children had all put on warm things once more, because it had become much colder as they went northwards.

They stood watching for their first glimpse of England. 'There, over there!' yelled Mike, suddenly, his sharp eyes catching a very faint line on the horizon. 'Oh Daddy, there's dear old England.'

He had a lump in his throat as he watched the faint line grow bigger and stronger. He seemed to know and love his own country much more now that he had been to others. He would always always love it best!

'Well, our trip is over,' said Granny's voice. 'And how lovely it has all been. How brown and well we are! And now children, school and hard work to make up all the weeks you have missed!'

'Yes,' said Belinda. 'I shall like going back. I'm ready for school now. What a lot we shall have to tell the others!'

'I hope we do Portugal and Spain and all the rest in geography this term,' said Mike. 'I feel I know a bit of *real* geography at last!'

England was clearly to be seen now. Mummy squeezed Daddy's hand. 'Home's all the nicer for having been away from it, isn't it?' she said. 'Dear old England! We're coming back to your autumn mists, your yellowing trees and falling leaves – and we're glad!'

'Won't it be fun to live in the caravans again, and see Davey and Clopper, and hear the rain on the caravan roof when we're cosily inside?' said Belinda.

'Oh hurry, *Pole Star* – we want to be home again!'

'There's no place like home!' sang Ann, suddenly. 'Goodbye, bulls and flying-fish and dolphins and diving boys and bullock-carts and monkeys – and smells! Goodbye! There's no place like home!'

The
Seaside
Family

Contents

1

Summer Holidays Again

'School's over for two months, thank goodness!' said Mike, and he slammed his books down on the table. The vase of flowers there nearly jumped off the table. 'Mike! Be careful,' said Mummy. 'There now – Belinda has done the same – and off goes the vase.'

'Sorry Mummy,' said Belinda, and picked up the vase. Mike went to get a cloth to wipe up the water. Ann picked up the flowers. They were all laughing. Mummy couldn't help laughing too.

'Well I know how you feel, when school is ended for a time,' she said. 'The summer holidays are so lovely and long for you too, aren't they – almost eight weeks. Goodness me – what shall I do with you for eight weeks?'

'I know what I want to do,' said Mike. 'I want to go to the seaside. We've been in a houseboat on a canal . . .'

'And we've been on a big ship for a trip,' said Ann.

'And now we want to go to the seaside,' said Mike. 'Don't we, girls?'

'Yes,' said the girls at once, and Mummy smiled.

'You've been planning this together on the way home from school!' she said. 'Well, it's no good asking *me*. It's Daddy you must ask. It costs money to go to the seaside, you know, and we don't have very much to spare.'

'Mummy, we don't see why it should cost very much to go and stay at the seaside,' said Mike, earnestly. 'Can't we go in our caravans? Then we don't need to take a house anywhere, or to go to a hotel. We'd just live in the caravans as usual.'

Mike's family had two caravans that stood in a green field where cows grazed. Sometimes the cows bumped against the vans at night and woke the children – but they didn't mind little things like that! That was all part of the fun.

The caravans were painted red and yellow. They had little red chimneys out of which smoke came when Mummy lighted her fire, or got the stove going in the children's caravan.

Mike, Belinda and Ann slept in three bunks, one above the other in one caravan. Mummy and Daddy slept in bunks in the other caravan. It was fun.

The children lived at school from Monday to Friday in the term-time, and came back to the caravans for the weekends. How they loved that! What fun it was to have a home on wheels, one that had no roots, but could be taken anywhere they liked.

'We'll ask Daddy as soon as we see him,' said Mike.

'We'll *make* him say yes. He'll love it too.'

So they lay in wait for Daddy, and hurled themselves on him as soon as he walked in at the field-gate.

'Daddy! We've something to ask you.'

'Something very important!'

'Something you've *got* to say yes to!'

'Is it something about the summer holidays?' asked Daddy thinking that three children could be very very heavy when they all hung on to him at once.

'Yes,' said everyone.

'Well, before you begin, let me break the news to you,' said Daddy firmly. 'Whatever ideas you've got in your head have got to come out. I've no money to spend on a summer holiday by the sea! That is – if you want to go to a hotel. The only thing I can do for you this summer is to let you go away somewhere fresh and new in the caravans. Nothing else at all.'

The three children squealed loudly.

'But *Daddy!* That's what we WANT! We want to go to the sea in the caravans. It's what we wanted to ask you.'

'Well, well, well – great minds certainly do think alike!' said Daddy. 'I must ask Mummy about it first.'

'We've asked her, we've asked her!' chanted Ann. 'And she said we must ask you. And we've asked *you*. So is it settled?'

Daddy began to laugh. 'What a lot of little pests you are! Yes, yes – it's settled. We'll choose a nice seaside place, and we'll all go off there together. I shall enjoy it too. But wait a minute – I've just thought of something.'

'What?' said all three alarmed.

'It's this – I've asked Ben Johns to come and stay with you here,' said Daddy. 'I meant to put him up in the farmer's cottage and let him play with you all day. Oh dear – what shall we do about that?'

By this time Mummy was with them. 'Oh – little Ben Johns?' she said. 'Yes, I remember we said we'd have him for a time. Poor child, his mother's very ill, isn't she? Well – we can't very well go to the seaside then.'

'We can! We can take him too!' said Belinda. 'Just another bunk put up in our caravan, that's all! We've three already. Can't you get another one just for these holidays, Daddy?'

'Yes – I suppose we could,' said Daddy, and everyone cheered. 'Now – I want my TEA! Who's going to get it? And afterwards we'll settle everything.'

'More fun!' cried Belinda, running to make the tea. 'More fun for the Caravan Family!'

2

Benjy Comes Along

It was great fun planning the seaside holiday. They got out maps and pored over them.

'Let's go to the east coast,' said Mummy. 'It's so healthy.'

'Too cold for me,' said Daddy, 'Let's go to the west coast.'

'What's this little place down here?' said Belinda, pointing to where a bit of land curved out and made a small bay. 'It looks lovely here – on the south coast.'

'That's Sea-gull Cove,' said Mike, reading the name printed in very small letters. 'What a lovely name!'

'Sea-gull Cove!' said Daddy, suddenly looking excited. 'Why, I know that. I went there three times when I was a small boy – just for the day only, it's true, but I never forgot it. It's the dearest little cove you ever saw.'

'Let's go there then,' said Mike, at once.

But Mummy wanted to know more about it. 'Is the bathing safe? Does the tide come in too fast? Is the beach sandy or shingly?'

'The bathing's safe, the tide comes in quickly, but

135

that doesn't matter, and the beach is golden sand – with shells all over it. Does that please you, Mummy?' said Daddy.

'And is there a good place for the caravans?' asked Mummy. 'Is there a farmhouse near for food? Is there . . .'

'Oh Mummy – just let's go, and we'll soon find out,' said Belinda. 'Sea-gull Cove – it sounds just right.'

'I'll pop down there and see if it's still as I remember it,' said Daddy. 'I'll go this week. In the meantime I'll arrange for another bunk to be put into the children's caravan for Benjy – he'll be coming tomorrow.'

The next day two men came along with some wood and went into the children's caravan. Mike, Belinda and Ann followed them in, staring. The caravan was quite crowded out then!

'We'll put the new bunk here – opposite the other bunks,' said the first man.

'Put it under the window, then Ben can look out,' said Belinda. 'Will it fold down to be out of the way in the daytime?'

'Oh yes,' said the man. 'Now – you'd better all get out of here, because when we start hammering and sawing we want a bit of space! My, these caravans are nice, aren't they? I wouldn't mind living in one myself. I suppose you wouldn't sell me this one, miss?'

'Oh *no*,' said Belinda. 'It's our home. We're the Caravan Family!'

'But we'll soon be the Seaside Family,' said Ann, going down the steps outside the caravan. 'Mike, Belinda – who's this? Is it Benjy?'

A small boy, a bit younger than Mike, was standing rather forlornly at the gate of the field, a large bag beside him. He was looking over at the caravans.

'Yes. It must be Benjy,' said Mike. None of the children had seen him before. He was just the son of a friend of Daddy's, and his mother was ill. That was all the children knew about him.

They went over to him. He didn't look very strong. He had straight fair hair and rather pale blue eyes, and a nice, sudden smile.

'Are you Benjy?' said Mike, and the boy nodded.

'Well, I'm Mike – and this is Belinda – and this is Ann – they're my sisters,' said Mike. 'Come along and I'll take you to our mother. You're going to live with us for a bit, aren't you?'

'In our caravan. And we're just getting a bunk put in for you,' said Belinda.

'Don't you think you're lucky to be going to live in our caravan – a house on wheels?' said Ann.

'Well – I don't know,' said Benjy. 'I always thought it was gipsies who did that. I don't know that I'm going to like it. I'd rather live in a house.'

This was such a surprising remark to the three

children that they stared at Benjy without a word. Ann felt cross. How could anyone possibly prefer a house to their colourful caravan?

Mike saw that Ann was going to say something that might sound rude to a visitor, so he spoke hurriedly.

'Come and see our mother. And I say – isn't it grand – we're all going off to the sea in two days' time!'

Ben's face brightened. 'Oh – that's better. We'll be in a hotel then, I suppose?'

'No. In our caravan,' said Ann. 'But if you don't like sleeping inside, you can sleep underneath!'

Benjy was just going to answer back when the children's mother came over to welcome him. She was so nice that Benjy was all smiles and politeness at once.

'You're just in time for a meal, Benjy,' she said. 'Such a nice one too – hard-boiled eggs and salad, and raspberries and cream! Will you like that?'

Benjy clearly thought that this was quite all right. Belinda pulled Ann aside. 'Oh dear – he'll *spoil* the holiday! How I do wish we were going by ourselves. And I'll hate him in our caravan! What a pity!'

3

Off to the Seaside

After their good meal of eggs and salad, raspberries and cream, the children went to show Benjy the caravan he was to share with them. The men had now put in the new bunk, and Mummy had put bedding on it. It looked very nice.

'Come on Benjy – we'll show you everything,' said Belinda. They all went into the caravan. Belinda ran up the steps first. She showed Benjy the door – it was cut in halves in the middle, so that you could have just the bottom half shut if you wanted to, and the top half open, or both halves shut at once to make a door.

The caravan looked so nice inside. It had highly polished cork carpet all over the floor, with red rugs on it. There was a little stove at one end for heating the caravan in winter. There was a small sink with taps, so that washing-up could be done.

'Isn't it marvellous, to have a sink and taps and water in a caravan?' said Ann, and she turned on a tap to show Benjy that real water came out. But he didn't think it was very wonderful.

'What's so grand about *that*?' he said. 'Water comes out of our taps at home too. I suppose you've got a water-tank on the roof, haven't you? Most caravans have.'

It was all very disappointing. Benjy hardly looked at the bunks. He patted his and made a face. 'A bit hard. Hope I shall sleep all right at night.'

'You ought to be thinking yourself jolly lucky to be sleeping in a bunk in a caravan,' said Ann, quite fiercely. Mike nudged her. This was Benjy's first day and he was still quite a new visitor. You didn't talk like that yet!

Nobody showed him the cupboards where things were kept so neatly. Nobody asked him to admire the row of cups and saucers and plates. Benjy didn't want to live in a caravan, so he wasn't going to admire anything about theirs at all. It was really very disappointing.

'You'll have to share our jobs,' said Mike, as they went down the caravan steps again. 'You know – help to get the wood in, and wash up . . .'

'And make your own bunk and keep it tidy,' said Belinda.

'Goodness – can't you girls make the bunks by yourselves?' asked Benjy, rather scornfully. 'That's not a boy's work – making beds.'

'Our Daddy often makes up his own bunk, and if he can do it, so can you,' said Ann at once, and

140

she put on a really terrible glare. Mummy was most astonished to see it when she met them round the corner of the caravan. Dear, dear – didn't her three want poor Benjy?

Two days went by very quickly. There was such a lot to do that the children didn't bother about Benjy and his ways very much. They had to go with their mother to buy beach clothes and swimming costumes, and they had to spend a day with Granny, who wanted to see them before they went. They had to go and fetch their two horses, Davey and Clopper, from the farmer, because they were to pull the caravans all the way to the sea.

Fortunately for Benjy he liked both Davey and Clopper! Ann really felt she might have smacked him if he had said something horrid about them.

'This is dear old Davey,' she said, patting the strong little black horse, that showed a white star on his forehead. 'He is awfully good and quiet – you can ride him.'

'And this is Clopper,' said Mike, leading up a dark brown and white horse. 'He's a very good horse – but he won't stand any nonsense. They're both darlings.'

'Oh, I like them,' said Benjy, and he stroked the velvety black nose that rested on his shoulder. 'Davey, I like you. And Clopper, you're a beauty. I love your shaggy feet. I say, Mike, let me drive your caravan, will you? I can make Clopper go as fast as anything.'

Daddy overheard him, 'Well, you won't drive old Clopper then,' he said, firmly. 'He's not a race horse! I shan't let you drive till I can trust you. Now, can you all be ready in an hour's time? I want to start for Sea-gull Cove then.'

Could they be ready? Of course they could! Ann was ready in five minutes! She could always be quick when she really wanted to. Mike got the horses into harness. They stood patiently between their shafts, glad to be on the move once more.

Belinda went round picking up every scrap of litter. Mummy would never let one tiny bit of paper, or even a bit of egg-shell, be left in the field. Every corner had to be tidy and neat.

At last they were all ready. Daddy got up on the driving-seat of Davey's caravan. 'I'll go first, Mike, and show the way,' he called. 'Follow after me. Benjy, wait and shut the gate behind us.'

They were off – off to Sea-gull Cove by the sea! First went Daddy's caravan, with good old Davey pulling it – and then came Clopper, driven by Mike, pulling the children's caravan.

'We shall soon be the Seaside Family!' sang Belinda. 'Hurrah, hurrah, for the Seaside Family on its way to Sea-gull Cove!'

4

Sea-gull Cove

It was exactly the right day to set off for the seaside. The sun shone down hotly, and the sky was bright blue except for little white clouds here and there.

'I'm sure those clouds are made of cotton wool,' said Ann, and that made everyone laugh. They really did look like puffs of wool.

Davey and Clopper went steadily down the country lanes. Daddy had looked up the best way to go on his big maps, and he had chosen the winding lanes rather than the main roads, because then they wouldn't meet so much traffic.

'And anyway the lanes are prettier than the roads,' said Belinda. 'I love the way the red poppies nod at us as we go by, and the blue chicory flowers shine like little stars.'

'It takes longer to go by the lanes, Daddy says,' said Ann. 'But who minds that? If it takes longer than a day we can easily take our caravans into a field for the night and camp there!'

'Dear me, yes,' said Benjy. 'I hadn't thought we could do that. That might be rather fun!'

'You couldn't do that with a house,' said Mike, clicking to Clopper. 'A house has to stay put. It hasn't got wheels it can go wandering away on for miles and miles.'

'Still – I do prefer a house,' said Benjy, obstinately. 'I say, Mike, you might let me drive Clopper for a bit now.'

'No,' said Mike, firmly. 'Daddy said you can't until he can trust you. I'm driving Clopper all day – unless I give the girls a turn.'

They went slowly down the little sunny lanes all day long. Daddy called a halt at teatime. 'We can't get to Sea-gull Cove today after all,' he said. 'We must camp in a meadow for the night. I can see a farmer over there. I'll ask him if we can stay here, in this field nearby.'

The farmer was nice. 'Yes, of course you can put up in my field,' he said. 'I can see you're the sort of folks I can trust not to set things on fire, or leave gates open. I'll send my boy out with eggs and milk, if you'd like them.'

They all spent a very happy evening in a field where big brown and white cows grazed, whisking their tails to keep away the flies.

'I wish I had a tail like a cow,' said Ann, flapping at the flies over her head. 'I think it would be so very very useful!'

Davey and Clopper kept together away from the

cows. They went to drink at the stream, and then they pulled at the juicy grass nearby. They looked happy and contented. They were tired after their long walk, pulling heavy caravans – and it was nice to eat and drink and rest in a shady green field.

Ann came to give them each a lump of sugar. Benjy went with her. The horses nuzzled him and Ann, and blew down Benjy's neck. He was delighted.

'I wish they were mine,' he said to Ann. 'Fancy having two horses of your own like this. You *are* lucky!'

'You're nice when you talk like that,' said Ann. 'Instead of turning up your nose at everything!'

'Ann! Benjy! I want you to come and get into your bunks!' called Mummy. 'We're going to start off very early tomorrow morning, at half-past six. Come along quickly.'

Everyone was fast asleep before it was dark that night, even Mummy and Daddy! They were tired with their long drive and the sun and the breeze. Nobody heard the cows bumping into the children's caravan in the middle of the night, nobody even heard the screech owl that screamed and made Davey and Clopper almost jump out of their skins!

Daddy was awake at six o'clock. He looked out of the open door of the caravan. What a perfect morning! The sun was up, but still rather low, and the shadows of the trees were very long. Dew lay heavily on the grass.

Soon the whole family was having breakfast. Mummy had boiled the eggs from the farm, and there was creamy milk, new bread and farm butter with homemade strawberry jam. Everyone but Benjy ate two eggs each.

'What a poor appetite you've got, Benjy!' said Ann. 'No wonder you look so pale.'

'*I* think you're greedy!' said Benjy. 'Two eggs for breakfast! *I* can't think how you manage to eat them!'

'You wait for a few days – then you'll be like Mike, asking for *three* eggs, not two!' said Belinda.

They set off once more in the caravans. Davey and Clopper plodded along steadily – clippity-clop, clippity-clop.

Up hill and down hill, along pretty valleys, round the honeysuckle hedges, past green woods – and then, what a surprise!

They rounded a corner on a hill – and there stretching below them was the sea – miles upon miles of brilliant blue water!

'Oh – the SEA!' yelled Ann, and all the children shouted for joy. The first sight was always so exciting.

'And there's Sea-gull Cove!' cried Mike, pointing. 'Look – it must be. Isn't it, Daddy?'

Yes, it was. There it lay, a little bay of yellow sand and blue sea. On the beach sat a crowd of sea-gulls. They rose into the air and came gliding over the children's heads, calling loudly.

'They're saying, "Welcome to Sea-gull Cove",' said Ann, pleased. 'They really are pleased to see us! Oh, what a lovely little place!'

5

Settling in at Sea-gull Cove

The caravans went slowly down the hill to Sea-gull Cove. It was a steep hill, and the road wound round and about. Daddy and Mike had to put on the brakes of the caravans or they would have run down the hill of their own accord and bumped the horses along too fast!

The cove looked nicer and nicer as they came nearer. 'The beach is simply *covered* with shells!' called Mike.

'And look at the rockpools shining blue,' said Belinda. 'How lovely to paddle in those. They'll be as warm as anything.'

'We can have baths every single day from morning to night,' said Ann.

'*I* shan't,' said Benjy at once. 'I'm not keen on bathing at all. Horrible cold water – and I can't swim, so I hate going in deep.'

'Can't *swim!*' said Ann, astonished. 'Why, I've been able to swim for ages and I'm much younger than you. You *are* a baby!'

Benjy went red and looked cross.

'Now he'll sulk,' said Belinda. 'Well, let him! He'll just *have* to learn to swim if he's going to enjoy himself here. My goodness, isn't the water blue!'

'Mike!' yelled back Daddy from his caravan in front. 'We'll take the caravans right down to the cove. There's a stretch of sandy grass at the back of the beach. If it's all right we'll have our caravans there.'

The children squealed for joy. 'Oh Daddy!' shouted Belinda, 'how glorious! Perhaps the tide will come almost up to our doors. We can leave them open and lie and look at the sea when we're in bed.'

The caravans were placed side by side on the little grassy stretch behind the beach. Davey and Clopper were led into a field behind. Daddy set off to talk to the farmer who owned the land nearby. He had already seen him when he had gone down to Seagull Cove for the day. He knew it was all right to put the horses there. Now he wanted to arrange for food and water for his little family.

The children raced on to the sandy beach. It was firm and golden beneath their bare feet. Ann picked up some of the shells. 'Look – as pink as a sunset! And do look at this one – it's like a little trumpet. Oh, I shall make a most beautiful collection of shells to take home with me!'

Belinda and Mike ran down to the edge of the sea. Little waves curled over each other just there, and ran up the smooth, shining sand. Farther out were bigger waves, curling over with little splashes. The children yelled for joy.

'We'll bathe all day! We'll paddle! We'll get a boat and row! We'll shrimp and we'll fish! We'll . . .'

Mike leapt into a bigger wave than usual and splashed Belinda from head to foot. Mummy called to him. 'Mike! If you're going to do that sort of thing come and get into swimming costumes! But first, don't you want something to eat?'

'Yes, if we can take it down to the very edge of the sea,' said Mike. He looked round for Benjy. Benjy was dabbling his toes in the edge of the water, looking rather solemn.

'Isn't it *lovely*, Benjy?' cried Belinda, rushing up to him, and giving him a little push that sent him running farther into the sea.

'Don't!' said Benjy, coming back in a hurry. 'My feet are awfully hot and the water's frightfully cold. I was just getting used to it.'

'I said, isn't it lovely!' cried Belinda, who was determined to make Benjy admire Sea-gull Cove.

'Well, it *looks* lovely – but won't it be rather lonely?' said Benjy. 'Shan't we be rather bored here all by ourselves?'

'Daddy says only stupid people are bored!' shouted Ann, in delight, coming up. 'So you must be stupid! Stupid baby!'

'Ann!' called Mummy, really shocked. 'Don't be so

rude to Benjy. Let him get used to things.'

'Well, he must get used to us too, then,' said Ann. 'Mummy, how *can* he ask if we'll be bored in this lovely, lovely place?'

'Ann,' said Mummy, pulling her quietly to one side. 'Do remember that Benjy is very fond of his mother, and I expect that, although he doesn't say much about it, he is secretly very worried about her – she is terribly ill, you know.'

'Oh dear,' said Ann. 'I quite forgot. I'm sorry, Mummy. I'll try and remember to be nice to him. All the same, he's a silly baby.'

Soon all four children were in their swimming costumes. Mummy gave them a basket of food to take down to the very edge of the sea.

'Let's go and sit in the water and have our dinner,' said Belinda, with a giggle. 'I've never in my life had a picnic sitting in the water.'

So they went and sat down in the edge of the sea – all except Benjy, who thought it was a horrid idea. They ate their ham sandwiches and nibbled their tomatoes happily, while tiny waves ran up their legs and all round their bodies.

'Lovely!' said Mike, popping the last of his tomato into his mouth. 'Hurrah for Sea-gull Cove – the nicest place in the world!'

6

Benjy has a Lesson

The tide came in all that afternoon. It crept up the beach bit by bit, and the children watched eagerly to see if it would reach the caravans. But it didn't of course.

'Do you think it might if we had a storm, Daddy?' asked Ann, longingly. 'Oh, Daddy – do you suppose the water would ever get to the top of the wheels, so that the two caravans would float away like Noah's Arks?'

'Oooh – that *would* be fun!' said Belinda.

'That would never happen,' said Daddy, firmly. 'Because if there were a storm I should at once move the caravans farther back!'

'Oh Daddy – you're a spoil-sport!' said Ann, with a laugh. 'Just think of us all floating gaily away on the sea!'

'How horrid!' said Benjy, with a shiver.

'Benjy's afraid of adventures,' said Ann. 'He doesn't even like going into the water up to his knees. He . . .'

'Ann!' said Mummy, sharply. 'Have you already forgotten what I said?'

Ann went red. 'Oh dear – I'm so sorry,' she said.

'Well, please don't forget again,' said Mummy. 'I don't like being cross on a holiday. Now, what are you going to do? Paddle, dig, bathe, or what?'

'Bathe,' said Mike, at once. 'I want a good long swim. Coming, Daddy?'

'Rather!' said Daddy, 'and Mummy will too. I'll give Benjy his first lesson in swimming too, I think.'

Benjy looked up in alarm. 'I don't think I want to learn to swim,' he said.

'Rubbish!' said Daddy. 'All children must learn to swim. Look at Ann here – she swims like a little fish.'

'I can even swim under water,' said Ann, proudly. 'It's easy! I can open my eyes under water too, and see the things on the bottom of the sand.'

'Can you really?' said Benjy, amazed. 'I should like to do that!' He turned to Ann's father. 'All right, sir, I'll do my best to learn. But don't duck me or anything, will you?'

'You can trust Daddy,' said Belinda, at once. 'He'll always tell you what he's going to do.'

So Benjy had his first lesson. He was afraid when he had to walk right into the water up to his waist. He said it was cold, he said it was too deep, he said he was sure there were crabs waiting to bite his toes!

'Yes, it does seem a bit cold,' agreed Daddy. 'And it is quite deep for you. And there may be one or two crabs. But we just won't bother about any of those things at all. Now then – bend forward – that's right – up with your legs! Don't struggle. I've got you safely. Can't you feel my hand under your tummy?'

Benjy really was very frightened, but he tried his best to do what Daddy said. He worked his arms and legs furiously, and got completely out of breath. The other children roared with laughter at him.

'Daddy, he's trying to go at sixty miles an hour!' squealed Ann. 'You'll have to give him a hooter or something if he goes at that pace!'

That made Benjy laugh too, and he swallowed a mouthful of water and choked. He struck out with his arms in alarm, and clung to Daddy quickly.

'There – you're all right and you did quite well,' said Daddy. 'Now walk into the shallower water while we all go out for a swim.'

Then the Caravan Family all went for a swim together. They went into deep water, and not even Daddy could feel the sand below with his feet. Ann felt very brave indeed. Then she gave a sudden scream and Daddy looked round at once.

'Oh! Oh! Something's nibbling me! OH!'

Daddy swum up to her and then he turned over on his back and roared with laughter as he floated there.

'Look what's nibbling Ann!' he shouted to the others, and he held up a strand of ribbon seaweed! 'It was bobbing against her – and she thought it was nibbling her! Oh, Ann – how does seaweed nibble?'

It was such fun in the water. But soon Daddy led the way back to the shore, striking out strongly. 'It's the first time we've been swimming for a long time,' he called. 'We won't overdo it – we shall be so stiff tomorrow if we do. Come along to the beach and we'll have some races to warm us up.'

They went to the sandy beach. Benjy was there waiting for them, shivering. Daddy made them all race up and down, up and down, and soon they were warm and glowing.

'The tide's almost up to the caravan steps, it is really, look!' cried Ann, in delight. Everyone looked. It was about twelve feet away from the steps, but the water was already going down. It certainly wouldn't reach the caravans *that* evening!

Belinda gave a terrific yawn. Mummy heard her. 'You're all tired out with excitement,' she said. 'We'll have a light supper – and then off to bed!'

Funnily enough nobody minded going to bed early. 'You see,' said Ann, 'it's going to be *such* a treat lying in our bunks, Mummy, and looking out at the evening sea – and watching it get darker and darker!'

But she didn't see it getting darker – she was sound asleep!

7

Everything is Lovely

Next morning Mike awoke first. He couldn't think what the noise was just outside. Lap-lap-lap, plish-plash-plash!

And then he remembered – of course, they were by the sea. THE SEA! He sat up in his bunk and looked out. The tide was in again, and was lapping some yards away from the caravan steps. Plish-plish-plash! The sun shone over the great stretch of water and made bright sparkles on it everywhere.

Mike took a deep breath. It was all so clean and new. Surely the world never never looked so lovely as it did in the very early morning.

There came a rush of big wings, and Mike saw a sea-gull standing in the edge of the water. It was facing the caravan. He held his breath because it began to walk towards the steps!

It was a magnificent bird, snow-white and pearl-grey with bright, alert eyes. It walked up to the caravan and then hopped up a step – then another step – then another! And at last it was on the top step of all, peering into the caravan, its head on one side!

'Eeee-ooo, eee-ooo, eee-ooo!' it screamed suddenly, as if it were asking for breakfast. Mike almost jumped out of his skin. The other three awoke in a fright and sat up. They stared in surprise at the enormous sea-gull. It flapped its great wings and soared away into the air. 'Eee-ooo, eee-ooo, eee-ooo!' it squealed, almost as if it were laughing at them.

'Goodness – that did scare me!' said Ann, with a laugh. 'Did it come to say good morning or what, Mike?'

'It's awfully tame,' said Mike. 'We'll feed the gulls today with bread, and see if we can get them to take it from our hands. I really thought that gull was going to walk into the caravan! I say – what about a bathe before breakfast?'

'Horrid!' said Benjy. But the others didn't think so and they scrambled into bathing things and tore down to the water at once. It was cold – but who minded that? Well, Benjy did, of course, but as he didn't put more than his toes into the water, he didn't even shiver.

Mummy called to him. 'Benjy – if you're not going to bathe, come and help me with breakfast. And you might see if you can find some driftwood on the beach, thrown up by the tide. We'll have to find some wood somewhere for the fire, and stack it in the sun to dry.'

Benjy had already found that there were plenty of

odd jobs to do if you lived in a caravan. He had learnt to make his own bed – or rather his bunk – each day. He had been ticked off for leaving the tap running so that the water-tank had emptied. He had had to sweep the floor several times and shake the mats.

He was beginning not to mind doing all these little jobs. Everyone else did them cheerfully, and after all they weren't very much bother. All the same he made up his mind that Mike would have to do his share of hunting for driftwood and bringing it to stack in the sun for the fire!

'I want to buy a boat to sail on the rockpools,' said Belinda at breakfast. They were having it on the beach. Daddy had lighted a wood-fire to boil the kettle and cook the eggs. 'Can I go to the nearest village and see if I can get one, Mummy?'

'And I want a shrimping-net,' said Mike. 'I bet I could catch enough shrimps to cook for tea each day!'

'Oooh, lovely,' said Belinda. 'I do like shrimps with brown bread and butter. Do *you* want to buy anything at the shops, Benjy?'

'I'll see,' said Benjy. 'I might buy a big ball if I can see one. This is a good beach for a ball.'

'And I shall buy ice-creams for everyone,' said Ann.

'We won't be *too* long at the village,' said Belinda. 'We simply mustn't waste a single hour away from Sea-gull Cove if we can help it. Mummy, can I throw some bread to the gulls now? You've got half a stale loaf there.'

The gulls were standing not far off, watching the children eating. Mummy broke the stale loaf into bits and gave it to the four children. One by one they threw bits to the gulls.

They came nearer and nearer, squealing angrily if one gull got too many pieces. They pecked one another if they thought one had been unfair. 'Just like naughty children,' said Mummy.

'You know, if we get the gulls much tamer than this, we'll have to lock up all our food,' said Daddy. 'They will be into the caravans before we know where we are! Hey you big fellow, that's my toe, not a bit of bread!'

'Well,' said Mummy, getting up and scaring off the gulls at once, 'it's time we cleared away. Mike, there is a bus you can catch up the hill there in half an hour's time. Girls, wash up for me. Boys, make the bunks and look for wood. I'm going to the farm for food.'

Soon the little family was busy about its tasks, chattering happily. 'Now for the bus!' said Mike at last. 'Come on, or we'll miss it! Run, Benjy, or you'll be left behind!'

8

Benjy's Ball

They just caught the bus nicely, and off they went, jolting through the country lanes to the nearest village of Minningly. It was a dear little place, with only four shops, a church, a chapel, and clusters of pretty thatched houses.

'It must be fun to live in a tiny place like this and know simply *everybody*,' said Ann. 'I should like that.'

'Look – there's a shop where we can buy what we want,' said Mike. 'It looks as if it sells simply *everything*!'

So it did. It was a little general shop, hung with all kinds of things inside and out – pails, kettles, rope, sou'westers, china, wire-netting, postcards, sweets, ships, toys – everything was there it seemed!

'Is there anything you *don't* sell?' Ann asked the little round woman who beamed at them from behind a counter piled high with yet more goods.

'Oh yes, miss,' she said. 'I don't sell rocking horses and I don't sell cuckoo clocks – so don't you go asking for them now, will you?'

Ann giggled. 'I wasn't going to,' she said. 'I really want to buy some ice-cream.'

'Ah, I've plenty of *that*!' said the plump little woman, and she took the lid from a big ice-cream container. She scooped yellow ice-cream into four cornets. It looked lovely. Ann paid her in delight.

'*Just* what we wanted!' she said. 'Can we look round your exciting shop while we eat them?'

'Of course – and you can poke into any of the corners you like,' said the shop-woman. 'There's no knowing what you might find!'

Belinda found just the ship she wanted – one with a nice heavy keel that looked as if it would help the ship to sail properly and not fall on its side. Mike found a splendid shrimping-net – a good strong one that wouldn't break if he pressed it too hard into the sand when he went shrimping.

And you should have seen the ball that Benjy bought! It really was the nicest the four had ever seen! It was blown up to make it very big and bouncy. It was striped in yellow and red and blue and was twice as big as a football!

'That's a lovely ball to play with in the sea,' said the little shop-woman, when Benjy paid her. 'It bobs on the water like a live thing.'

'Oh, I shan't play with it on the sea,' said Benjy, at once. 'It's too precious. I shall only play with it on the sands.'

'I say – we'd better hurry if we want to catch the bus back,' said Mike, suddenly. 'Look – it's at the corner there, waiting. Goodbye – we did enjoy your shop!'

Off they went, scurrying to the bus, and it was not long before they were back at dear old Sea-gull Cove again. Daddy was waiting for them.

'Coming in for a bathe?' he shouted. 'And what about your swimming lesson, Benjy? You'll get on fine today!'

'I don't think I want one today,' said Benjy. 'I think I'd rather play with my new ball – isn't it a beauty?'

'Rather!' said Daddy. 'You can play with it after your lesson – we all will, to get ourselves warm. Come along now, into your swimming trunks!'

And so Benjy had his second lesson, and he splashed away valiantly. Daddy was quite pleased with him. 'Now listen to me, Benjy,' he said. 'You want to practise the strokes I have told you. Practise them by yourself in the water each day – three or four times a day.'

'Benjy won't! He never goes in farther than his knees!' shouted Ann. 'He's afraid!'

'Well – if he does not go in farther than that it'll take him a long time to learn to swim!' said Daddy. 'Now come on out, all of you – and we'll have a fine game with Benjy's new ball!'

It certainly was a lovely ball. It bounced as lightly as a feather, and was so light that even the wind could bowl it over the sand. The children had to run fast after it when the breeze began to join in their game!

They were all terribly hungry for dinner. Mummy had bought a big meat pie from the farm, and it was soon gone. Not even a small piece was left for the gulls! Then plums and greengages were handed out, and if anyone wanted bread-and-butter with them they could have it. Creamy milk from the farm was in a big jug set in a pail of cold water to keep it cool.

'Lovely!' said Ann, when she had finished. 'Now for another bathe.'

'Not after that enormous lunch,' said Mummy firmly. 'You can bathe at three o'clock, but not before. Have a read now, in the shade. That would be nice. Lend Benjy a book.'

At three o'clock Mike, Ann, Daddy, Mummy and Belinda were all out in the water again – they really were a family of fishes! Benjy wouldn't come. He played on the beach with his ball.

And then something happened. The wind took the big ball and blew it down to the edge of the sea. It bobbed on the water. It was taken out a little way. Benjy splashed in after it – but the wind took it out even farther! 'Mike! Belinda! Get my ball!' squealed Benjy. But nobody heard him, nobody at all.

Now what was he to do? He would lose his ball – there it went, bobbing away on the waves! Poor Benjy!

9

Benjy is Most Surprising

Benjy stood in the water up to his knees and howled dismally. 'My ball! Get my ball! It's going away on the water. MIKE! MIKE!'

But Mike didn't hear him. Mike was trying to swim under water with Ann. Daddy and Mummy were having a race on their own. Belinda was floating peacefully on her back. Nobody saw what was happening to Benjy.

Benjy stared desperately at his bobbing ball. It came back a little way because a wave broke over it and sent it rolling in towards the beach. If only it would come back a little more Benjy might be able to reach it.

He waded in deeper. Oooh – he was up to his waist now. How dangerous, he thought – and how cold! Ah, there was his ball – nearer still! Another few steps and he really might get it. He waded deeper still. Now he was almost up to it – and oh joy, a wave sent the ball almost on top of him. He had it! It was safe!

He felt very proud indeed. He had never been out so deep before. A wave wetted him right to the armpits. After all, the water wasn't so very cold – it was rather warm and felt silky to the skin. He waded back with his ball and put it in a safe place. Then he turned and looked at the sea.

The others were really having a glorious time out there. It was fun to hear them shouting and laughing. What a pity he couldn't swim!

Benjy waded into the sea again. It still felt warm. He waded right up to his waist. Then he bobbed under to wet his shoulders. Why, it was *lovely*! He stayed under for a little while and then began to make the armstrokes he had been shown that morning.

He suddenly lost his balance and his legs went up into the water. He struck out in alarm – and goodness gracious, he really could hardly believe it, but he swam three whole strokes before water went into his mouth and he choked!

Benjy was full of pride and amazement. He had swum – he really had! His feet had been right up in the water. Should he try again?

And then he saw the others nearby watching him in astonishment.

'Benjy! We saw you then! Were you really swimming?' yelled Ann.

'Benjy, do it again!' shouted Mike, swimming up. 'I say – you didn't *really* swim, did you?'

'I did,' said Benjy. 'I'll show you!'

He let his legs leave the sandy bottom and then

he struck out again. Four strokes this time before he went under, spluttering and gasping.

'Daddy, he's marvellous!' cried Belinda. 'Mummy, look, he's learnt already! If he practises he'll soon be swimming out with us! How lovely!'

Benjy had never felt so proud in his life. He had always been a spoilt timid boy – now for the first time he had been really brave on his own, and he felt grand. He did some more strokes, and then went under so completely that he really thought he was drowning!

'We're going in now,' said Mike helping him up to the surface. 'I say – don't swallow *all* the sea, will you? We do want a bit left, you know.'

'Can we play with your lovely ball, Benjy?' asked Ann, wading out with the spluttering Benjy.

'Yes, of course,' said Benjy.

'Benjy, whatever made you go and swim like that all by yourself?' asked Belinda curiously. 'I never thought you would. You *are* brave!'

Benjy nearly didn't say anything about his runaway ball. He badly wanted to be thought brave enough to go and practise all on his own, without any ball to make him wade into the water.

But he knew that Mike and the others always owned up and never pretended, and he wanted to be the same. So he went red and told them what had happened.

'I wasn't really brave! It was my new ball that made me go into the water. The wind blew it out to sea, and you didn't hear me calling to you to get it for me. So I waded out and got it – and it was so nice out there I thought I'd practise swimming. That's all. I wasn't really *brave*, you see.'

Daddy had heard all this. He clapped Benjy on the shoulder. 'It's nice to see a boy brave enough to own up that it was his ball sent him into the water, and nothing else – and very nice to see that he was sensible enough to stay there once he was in! I'm pleased with you Benjy. You'll be as fine a swimmer as Mike soon!'

Well, of course that was quite enough to make Benjy determined to practise his swimming every single day. He blushed with pride and thought the children's father was the nicest he'd ever met – except his own, of course.

They all had great fun that day. They sailed Belinda's boat on the pool, and it really did sail beautifully and only fell over once on its side, when the wind blew too strongly.

Mike went shrimping and caught seventy-two shrimps and Mummy cooked them for supper. The gulls came round and ate up all the heads and tails that nobody wanted!

'They're quite useful, aren't they?' said Ann, throwing them a few more heads from her plate.

'Good as dustmen, the way they clear up our litter! No, shoo, gull – you are *not* to peck Belinda's boat!'

'What fun we're having!' said Mike. 'I wish these holidays would never, never end!'

10

Ann and Benjy

Now the days began to slip by too quickly. 'I never know *what* day of the week it is now,' said Mike. 'I really thought today was Tuesday – and now I find it's Friday! Goodness knows where Wednesday and Thursday went to!'

'We know when it's Sunday, anyway,' said Ann, 'because then we hear the church bell ringing from the village of Minningly – and we go to church.'

'Yes – I liked that,' said Belinda. 'It's the dearest little church I ever went into – the sort of church that God really does feel near in.'

'We never go to church at home,' said Benjy, 'but I liked going with you. God never feels very near to me though. I'm sure He doesn't bother about a boy like me. I say "Our Father" at night, but I never ask Him for things like you do. I can't really feel that He's listening.'

'Well, you can't feel very safe then,' said Ann. 'I mean – we always feel that God really *is* a Father and loves us, and is always looking after us, so we feel safe. But you can't feel at all safe.'

'Well, I don't,' said Benjy. 'I'm always afraid something awful is going to happen, and – well, don't let's talk about it.'

'But I want to,' said Ann. 'Mike and Belinda, you go away. I do really want to talk to Benjy. I don't like his not feeling safe.'

Mike and Belinda went off. They were rather bored with this anyway. They just thought Benjy was being silly, as usual.

But he wasn't. Something was frightening him very much. He told Ann what it was.

'It's my mother,' he said. 'You know she's awfully ill, Ann. I haven't always been very kind to her, and now what's worrying me all the time is that she might – she might *die*, Ann, and I wouldn't even have been able to tell her I was sorry.'

'Oh Benjy!' said Ann. 'Might she really die? And you're away here with us and can't even tell her you love her and didn't ever mean to be horrid? Oh Benjy, I'm sorry I've been horrid to *you*. I ought to have been kind. I shall pray for ever so long tonight to ask God to make your mother better. You must too. God will know it's very important if we both pray for exactly the same thing for a long time.'

'Well, I will,' said Benjy. 'Don't tell your father and mother about this, Ann. You see, I heard them talking yesterday when they didn't know I was near – and they said my mother was worse. I couldn't help hearing.'

'Ann! Benjy! Whatever are you talking about so earnestly?' called Mummy. 'Not planning any mischief, I hope!'

'No, Mummy,' said Ann. She gave Benjy a quick hug. 'Don't worry any more. You needn't now.'

'ANN! Come on – Daddy's got a boat and we're going out on it!' shouted Mike. 'Do come.'

Ann was thrilled. She raced down to the sea, where Daddy had the boat. Benjy went too, looking much more cheerful. He hadn't liked Ann a bit before – but now he felt as if she was his best friend. He got into the boat with the others.

'Can you row?' Mike asked him. Benjy shook his head.

'But I'd like to learn,' he said, rather surprisingly.

'Good boy!' said Mike, and grinned at him. 'You're not nearly such a mutt as you were, are you?'

Rowing was hard work, Benjy found. All the others rowed well, even Ann. It really was astonishing, the things these three could do! They were always willing to try anything and go on trying till they were good at it.

They had a bathe from the boat itself. 'Ooooh! *Really* deep water here!' said Mike, and dived over the edge of the boat. Splash! He was up again at once. Belinda dived in too, but Ann let herself down over the side. Benjy looked at Anne's father.

'Shall I go in too, sir?'

'Yes, if you like,' said the children's father. 'If you get into trouble I'll dive in and get you. You can swim now – it doesn't matter whether you're in deep or shallow water, you can still swim!'

So in went Benjy, and although it gave him an odd feeling at first to know that the bottom of the sea was rather far down, he soon forgot it. He forgot his troubles too, and Ann was very pleased to hear him squealing with laughter.

Then back they went to the shore again, and the day slipped by as quickly as usual. It seemed no time at all before it was bedtime.

Benjy and Ann were sent to bed first because they were the youngest. 'Hurry, Benjy,' said Ann. 'Then we can have a long time to say our prayers before the others come. You know how important it is tonight.'

And so, if Ann's mother had looked in ten minutes later she would have seen two washed and brushed children kneeling down beside one of the bunks, absolutely still. How hard they were praying!

'Please, dear God, think how sad Benjy is and make his mother better,' prayed Ann. 'You always want to be kind, so I know You'll help poor Benjy. Please, please make his mother better!'

It was the longest prayer Benjy and Ann had ever made. 'Goodnight, Benjy,' said Ann, when she climbed into her bunk. 'God was listening, as he always does. Here come the other two – we only *just* finished in time!'

11

About Sea-creatures – and a Telegram!

Next day Benjy waited eagerly for the postman. Would there be good news? He had no letter, but there was one for the children's mother.

'Yes, Benjy,' she said, when she saw him looking anxiously at her. 'It's about your mother. She's just the same, neither better nor worse.'

'There you are,' Benjy said miserably to Ann, when they were alone. 'I told you so. God doesn't really care about a boy like me.'

'It's wicked to say things like that,' said Ann. 'Don't let's talk about it if that's what you think. Look, what's that – it's a starfish! Daddy, come and look!'

Everyone came and looked at the unusual five-fingered creature. 'It's just five legs and a tummy!' said Daddy. 'Its mouth is in the middle of it.'

'How does it get along?' asked Mike, seeing the creature dragging itself down the sand.

Daddy turned it over. The children saw dozens of white tube-like things sticking out of the five fingers. 'Those are its legs,' said Daddy. 'Look at the way it puts them out. It takes hold of the ground with the first rows, pulls itself up, takes hold with the back legs, and so it gets along. Very clever!'

The starfish got into a pool and disappeared. A crab ran out as if it was afraid. It sank itself into the soft wet sand and vanished.

'That's another clever little creature!' said Mike, with a laugh. 'I wish I could make myself disappear like that. Daddy, how do crabs grow? Their hard shell can't grow, surely?'

'Oh no,' said Daddy. 'The poor crab has to creep into a dark corner and hide himself when he grows too big for his shell. Then his shell splits – and out he wriggles! He hides away quietly for a day or two – and hey presto, a completely new shell grows on his body!'

'It's just like magic,' said Ann. 'I wish I could see it happening. Daddy, I'm going shrimping if Mike will let me borrow his net. Then you can tell me about shrimps and prawns too!'

She went off with Mike's net, and soon she and Benjy were hard at work catching shrimps and prawns in the big rockpools.

They looked at their peculiar eyes on stalks, and their funny little bunches of swimmeret legs. 'Daddy told me that the shrimps and prawns are the dustmen of these rockpools.' said Ann. 'They clear up all the rubbish. Did you know that, Benjy? Oh, do look – there are some sea-anemones!'

They both looked at the different jelly-like lumps growing in red and green on the rock in the water. 'Watch!' said Ann. 'They will put out things that look like petals soon, and wave them about in the water. Mummy, look! What are those sea-anemones doing?'

'Ah, they are trying to trap tiny shrimps or other creatures in those waving petals,' said Mummy. 'Once they have caught them with those unusual arms of theirs they will drag them into their middles – and that's the end of the little shrimps! They're not flowers, of course, they are jelly-like creatures that are always hungry!'

'Can I give this one a bit of bread?' asked Ann. 'Here you are, anemone. Take that! Mummy, he's got it – his petals caught hold of it – and he's dragged it into his middle part. Goodness, I'm glad I'm not a shrimp in this pool!'

'Yes, it would be dangerous,' agreed Benjy, and he gently touched the petals of the sea-anemone. 'I can feel this one catching hold of my finger! No, anemone – you're not going to gobble it up!'

The day went quickly by and soon it was teatime. Belinda set the tablecloth out on the beach, and she and Ann put out the tea – two loaves of new bread, a big slab of farm butter, a chocolate cake from the farm, made that morning, and an enormous jar of homemade jam. What a tea!

They all sat down to enjoy it. In the middle of it

Benjy looked, and gave an exclamation.

'The telegraph boy! Oh dear – do you think he wants *us*?'

Everyone's heart sank. Daddy and Mummy looked at one another. They were afraid of what the telegram might say.

Poor Benjy went very pale. Ann squeezed his arm. 'It's all right,' she said. 'You'll see, it will be all right.'

The boy came up on his bicycle. Daddy took the telegram. Everyone watched him tear it open, his face grave. Then he suddenly smiled.

'Benjy! Your mother's better! She'll get well!'

'Oh!' squealed all the children, and Benjy sat smiling with tears running down his cheeks.

'You do look funny, Benjy, smiling and crying too,' said Ann. 'Oh, Benjy, I was right, wasn't I? Benjy, I'm so glad for you. Mummy, do look at him – I've never seen anyone laughing and crying at once before.'

'Don't be horrid, Ann,' said Mike.

'She's not,' said Benjy, in a shaky voice. 'You don't know how good and kind she is. It's all because of Ann that I'm happy again. Now I shall *really* enjoy my holiday!'

12

Goodbye to Sea-gull Cove!

Benjy was so full of high spirits after the good news that he made everyone laugh. He shouted, he paddled up to his waist, he turned head-over-heels in the water, he even swam fifty strokes out to sea and back, a thing he had never done before.

'Poor Benjy,' said Mummy, watching him. 'He must have been very miserable about his mother – and we didn't guess it.'

'Ann knew,' said Mike. 'Good old Ann. Hallo, here comes Benjy again, with his ball. All right Benjy, I'll play with you. Race you to the cliff and back, kicking the ball all the way!'

Benjy didn't say much to Ann about his feelings, because he was shy. 'I just want to say that I feel as if God's given me another chance now,' he said. 'I shall be awfully good to my mother to make up for my horridness before. Ann – wasn't it marvellous that our prayers were answered like that?'

'Yes, but I really did believe they would be,' said Ann. 'And that's important too, Benjy, don't forget. Benjy, do you like living in a caravan now? You didn't at first.'

'I love it,' said Benjy, promptly.

'Do you like sleeping in a bunk?' asked Ann.

'I love it,' said Benjy.

'Do you mind making the bunks and getting in the wood and things like that?' went on Ann.

'I love it,' said Benjy. 'Go on, I shall say "I love it" to everything you ask me, silly – don't you know I'm happy here?'

'Do you like polishing the floor of our caravan?' asked Ann, slyly. This was always her job.

'I love it,' said Benjy, of course.

'All right – you go and do it then for a change!' squealed Ann. And oddly enough, Benjy took the polishing duster and went off like a lamb. Well, well – he really was a different boy, there was no doubt about that!

And now the holidays really did seem to fly past. There were two days of rain, when the children sat and played games in the caravan and really enjoyed the change. They bathed in the rain too, and that was fun. There was one day that was so hot that nobody dared to sit out in the sun, and Ann expected to see the sea begin to boil! But fortunately it didn't!

Benjy astonished everyone by his sudden appetite. He demanded two eggs at breakfast-time – and one day he asked for three!

'Aha!' said Mummy, 'what did I tell you? Yes, you

can have another – but don't ask for *four* tomorrow, or there won't be enough.'

Then the last week came. Then the day before the last, when the children did simply everything they could so as not to miss anything.

'We'll dig and paddle and bathe and sail the little boat, and shrimp and go rowing and collect shells and seaweed,' said Belinda. 'Oh, I do hate it when holidays come to an end – it's just as horrid as the beginning is nice!'

And then the last day came. Oh dear! Come along Davey and Clopper, your holiday is over too. What – you are glad? You want to get back to the old field you know so well – you will enjoy the long pull home?

Seaweed hung in long strips from the outside walls of the caravans. The children were taking the fronds home to tell the weather.

'If the seaweed's dry the weather will be fine; if it gets damp, it shows rain is coming,' said Ann to Benjy. 'You can take the very nicest bits home with you to show your mother, Benjy.'

'I've had a lovely time,' said Benjy. 'I thought at first I was going to hate it, and I didn't much like any of you – but I've loved it, and I feel as if you were my very best friends.'

Then Mike made them jump. 'Football!' he said suddenly. 'I've just remembered – it'll be the Christmas term now, with football. And there'll be gym. I like that.'

'And we shall have hockey,' said Belinda. 'And we're going to do a play – aren't we Ann? We're both going to be in one at school.'

Everyone suddenly cheered up. Holidays were lovely – but there were things at school that you didn't have at any other time. There were so many others there too – there was always something going on. It would be fun to go back.

Davey and Clopper were put into the shafts. Daddy called to Benjy. 'You and Mike can take it in turns to drive Clopper, Benjy. I can trust you all right now.'

'I can trust you all right now.' What lovely words to hear. It was the nicest thing in the world to be trusted. Benjy would see that his mother could trust him now, too. He looked round at the golden beach. He was sad to leave it – but all good things come to an end.

'Come on, Benjy!' called Mike. 'We're going.'

Up the hill went the two caravans, pulled by good old Davey and Clopper. The sea-gulls came swooping round them. 'Eee-ooo, eee-ooo, eee-oooo!' they called.

'They're shouting goodbye,' said Ann, in delight. 'Goodbye! We'll come again. Don't forget us, will you, because we'll come again. Goodbye!'

The
Queen Elizabeth
Family

Contents

1

Home for the Weekend

'Cuckoo!' called Belinda, Mike and Ann, as they opened the gate leading into a field.

'Cuckoo!' called back their mother, waving to them from the steps of one of the colourful caravans there. 'So glad you're back again!'

It was Friday afternoon. Mike, Belinda and Ann went to board at school all the week – but they came back to their caravan homes for the weekend. How they liked that!

'It's such fun to have school-life from Mondays to Fridays – and then home-life in our caravans from Fridays to Mondays,' said Belinda, as they walked over to the two pretty caravans. Then Ann ran on in front and hugged her mother.

'Mummy – I was top in writing!' she said.

'And I got one of my drawings pinned up on the wall,' said Belinda, proudly. 'I couldn't bring it home because it's got to stay there all next week.'

'And what about you, Mike?' asked his mother.

Mike grinned. 'Oh – I shot three goals yesterday afternoon,' he said. 'So our side won.'

'What a very successful week!' said Mummy, and she sounded pleased. 'Well – I expect you'd like to know what I've done too. I've made new curtains for your caravan – and I've made some lovely blackberry jelly!'

'Top marks, Mummy!' said Mike, and hugged her. 'Are we having the jelly for tea?'

'We are,' said his mother, and led the way into her caravan. There was one caravan for her and Daddy and one for the three children. Mummy had laid tea in her caravan, and it looked lovely. Blackberry jelly, cream in a little jug, new bread and butter, ginger biscuits, a chocolate cake and tiny buns made by their mother.

'Nicest tea in the world,' said Mike, and sat down at once.

'You must go and wash your hands,' said Ann. 'Just look at them!'

'My hands are clean, and anyway I only go if Mummy tells me,' said Mike at once. 'Wash your own!'

'Where's Daddy?' asked Belinda. 'Will he be late or early?'

'Late,' said Mummy. 'His firm is doing a lot of business with America just now, and he has to have a good many meetings with the men who are going over there.'

'I wish *we* could go to America,' said Belinda. 'We're

learning about it in Geography. Did you know you had to cross an enormous ocean called the Atlantic, Mummy, to get to America?'

'Well, yes, I did happen to know that,' said Mummy, pouring out mugs of milk.

'And did you know that there are two great ships called the *Queen Elizabeth* and the *Queen Mary*, that go across it in just a few days?' asked Ann. 'Goodness, how I'd like to go in one. They're supposed to be the finest ships in the world.'

'They are,' said Mummy. 'Well, perhaps one day we will all go to America, and you'll see what it's like.'

'Only if we could come back afterwards,' said Mike suddenly. 'I expect I'd like America very much – but I should always, always like England best.'

'Well, of course,' said Mummy. 'All the same you'd be astonished to see the food the Americans have – much better than ours!'

'But I don't think there could be a nicer tea than this,' said Ann at once, with her mouth full of bread and butter and blackberry jelly and cream.

Mummy laughed. 'Well, so long as you're satisfied, that's all right. Now – save some of the cream for Daddy. I've made him a blackberry tart for his supper, and he likes to pour cream all over it!'

'He'll get fat,' said Belinda. 'Why – here he is!'

And sure enough, there he was, coming in at the field-gate, waving to his little family, who were now crowding out of the caravan to meet him.

'Daddy!' yelled Ann, and almost fell down the steps. Mike reached him first. Daddy always liked his Friday welcome. He said he felt such an important person when four people rushed at top speed to meet him!

'Why are you home early?' asked Mike. 'Mummy said you'd be late.'

'I'm home early for a very important reason,' said Daddy. 'I've got an invitation for you all to see the *Queen Elizabeth* tomorrow! She's at Southampton, and sails on Saturday night. How would you like to have tea on board?'

'Daddy! *Really*?'

'Oh, how super!'

'It can't be true!'

Everyone spoke at once, and Daddy put his hands over his ears. 'Good gracious, I shall be deaf. It really *is* true. Look – here are the cards. We get on board with these, and we can see over quite a lot of the ship – and have tea on board too.'

'Did you say tomorrow?' said Mummy. 'That will be *lovely*! What a good thing it's Saturday and the children are home. It would have been so disappointing if it had been on a school-day. How are we going?'

'I rang up Granny and she's lending us her car,' said Daddy. 'She wants to come too. So do you think you could take Ann on your knee in front, Mummy, and let Granny go behind with Mike and Belinda.'

'Oh, easily,' said Mummy. 'It would be lovely to have Granny too. What a treat! The children will hardly believe a ship can be as big as the *Queen Elizabeth*!'

'I shall never go to sleep tonight,' said Belinda, and the others said the same. But when bedtime came they were all as sleepy as usual, of course.

Mummy came into their caravan to kiss them goodnight.

'I do like the new curtains,' said Belinda sleepily. 'Thank you, Mummy, for making them. They're all over buttercups and daisies and cornflowers and marigolds. It's like looking at a field.'

Ann kissed her mother goodnight too. 'Mummy,' she said, in her ear, 'the ship won't sail off with us on board, will it? It'll wait till we've gone, won't it?'

'Oh yes – don't you worry about that!' said Mummy. 'Go to sleep now, and the morning will come all the sooner. You're going to have a really lovely day!'

2

A Very Big Ship

Mike woke first the next morning, and he remembered at once that it was Saturday – and that they were all going to see the big ship, *Queen Elizabeth*. He sat up and rubbed his hands in joy.

'Wake up, girls! It's *Queen Elizabeth* day!' he called, and Belinda and Ann woke with a jump. They too remembered what was going to happen, and they leapt out of their comfortable little bunks like rabbits springing from their holes.

Belinda flew down the steps of the caravan to help with the breakfast. Mike ran to see if there was plenty of wood for the fire. Ann made the bunks very neatly and tidily. There wouldn't be much time for jobs after breakfast today!

They didn't even have time to wash up the breakfast things before Granny's car arrived at the field-gate! 'Honk! honk!' the horn sounded. 'Honk, honk!'

'There's the car!' cried Ann, in excitement, and nearly knocked the milk over. 'Mummy, Mummy, we aren't ready!'

'Well, we soon shall be – but not if you knock

everything over,' said Mummy. 'Belinda, just pack all the things into the little sink so that we can wash them when we come back. Ann, Mike, go and get your hats and coats.'

Soon everyone was running over to the field-gate. Granny was in the car, looking out anxiously for them. Daddy opened the door and gave her a kiss.

'Hallo, hallo!' he said. 'Punctual as always. Good-morning, James. I hear you are going to be good enough to look after the caravans and the two horses for me today.'

The driver touched his cap. 'Yes, sir, I'd be delighted. Nice to have a day in a caravan in the country! And I'll see to the horses, sir. Davey and Clopper, aren't they?'

'Yes,' said the children. Ann touched his arm. 'You *will* go and talk to them, won't you?' she asked. 'They don't like it when we all go off for the day and nobody comes near them.'

'Don't you worry, miss – I'll ask them all their news,' said the driver, and he helped Mummy into the front seat.

Daddy got into the driving-seat. Ann sat on Mummy's knee in front. Mike and Belinda got in at the back, trying hard not to squash Granny too much. But she was a very little person and didn't really take up much more room than they did.

'Well, what a treat this is going to be!' said Granny.

'I was so surprised when Daddy rang me up last night. I've always wanted to see the *Queen Elizabeth* – our most magnificent ship!'

This time they drove the whole way to Southampton. They stopped for lunch, sitting in the sun on a grassy hillside, looking down over a valley. Little fields separated by green hedges spread out before them.

'It's rather like a patchwork quilt,' said Belinda. 'All bits and pieces joined together by hedges. Is America like this, I wonder?'

'Oh no!' said Daddy. 'You wouldn't see any tiny fields like this, with hedges between. You'd see miles upon miles of great rolling fields, as far as the eye can reach. One field in America would take a hundred of our little fields – sometimes a thousand or more!'

'It must be a very, very big country then,' said Ann. 'I should get lost in it.'

'You probably would!' said Granny. 'But as you're not going, you can feel quite safe here with me. Now – have we all finished our lunch? We ought to be setting off again.'

After a while they arrived at a big, familiar town. 'It's the port of Southampton,' Daddy declared, 'where big ships – and little ships too – come to harbour.'

'What a lot of cranes everywhere!' said Mike, watching a crane in the distance pulling up a great package. 'I suppose they're used to unload ships, aren't they?'

'Yes,' said Daddy. 'Do you see that little box-like house near the bottom of the crane? Well, a man sits in there all day long, and works the crane.'

'I'd rather like to do that,' said Mike. 'I once built a little crane with my Meccano, and it worked just like that big one.'

'Look! Aren't those the funnels of the *Queen Elizabeth*?' suddenly said Mummy, and she pointed beyond the crane. Daddy slowed down the car.

Two enormous red funnels showed above the tops of the buildings beyond the crane. 'Yes,' said Daddy. 'That's the *Queen Elizabeth*.'

The children stared in awe. She was even bigger than they remembered from their holiday on the *Pole Star*. 'Are those her *funnels*?' said Ann, hardly believing her eyes. 'Good gracious – if her *funnels* are higher than houses, what a *very* big ship she must be! Why, you could almost drop a house down one of her funnels!'

'Not quite,' said Mummy. The car went on again through the crowded streets of Southampton, and at last came to the docks. What a wonderful place!

Mike couldn't take his eyes from the ships there. Great big ships – smaller ships – quite small ships. Fussy little tugs bustling here and there. Boats everywhere. Hootings and sirens, and hammerings and shouts! What a wonderful place to live!

'I wish we lived at Southampton,' said Mike. 'I'd be down at the docks every day. I think I shall be a sailor when I grow up, Daddy.'

'Not an engine-driver after all?' said Daddy, stopping the car at a gate, and showing some tickets to the policeman there. 'Can we go through? Thank you.'

'The *Queen* is up beyond,' said the policeman, and saluted.

The car ran through the gateway, and Daddy put it in a parking-place where there were many other cars. Then they made their way to the *Queen Elizabeth*.

Ann didn't even know the *Elizabeth* when they came in sight of her. She hadn't expected anything so enormous. But the other two children gasped in surprise.

'Mummy! She's the biggest ship that was ever built!' cried Mike, as his eyes went up and up the sides of the great ship, past deck after deck, to the topmost one of all – then to the funnels that now towered far above him, higher than any house.

'She's grand,' said Daddy, proudly. 'I'm glad she's British. No one can beat us at ship-building. We've been ship-builders for centuries – and here's our grandest ship so far!'

'Let's go aboard – oh, do let's hurry up and go aboard!' cried Belinda. 'I want to see what she's like inside!'

3

Tea on the *Queen Elizabeth*

'Gangway for the *Queen Elizabeth*, sir? That one over there,' said a nearby sailor, and pointed to where a slanting gangway ran from the ship to the dock-side. Up they all went, and into the ship.

'We have to find Mr Harrison,' said Daddy, looking at his tickets. 'He will show us as much as he can.'

Mr Harrison was a very jolly man indeed. He wore officer's uniform, and greeted Daddy like an old friend.

'Good afternoon, sir. I was told you were coming. Now, how would you like to see over our little ship?'

Well, of course, it was anything but a little ship! The children were soon quite bewildered by all the different decks they were taken on – each deck seemed to stretch for miles! They went on the games deck too, and Mike wished they could have some games.

'Deck-tennis – ooh,' he said. 'And quoits – and shuffle-board. Oh Daddy, do people have time to play all these games on the way to America? There's such a lot of them.'

'Plenty of time,' said Daddy. 'Look – these are the lifeboats, slung up there ready for any emergency.'

'What's an emergency?' asked Ann.

'Oh – something like a terrible storm that might harm the ship and make it necessary for people to get off her in the lifeboats,' said Daddy. 'Or a fire aboard. You never know. All big ships have lifeboats.'

'Daddy, I can't somehow think that we're on a ship,' said Belinda, as they walked down another big deck. 'It's so very big. Why, when I look over the deck-rail the ships down below look like toys!'

'And we can't feel any movement either, because the ship's too big to feel any waves in the dock,' said Mike. 'I'd like to feel what it's like when she rolls, though – or don't big ships like this roll?'

'My word, young man, you wouldn't like it if you were on board when the *Elizabeth* really *does* roll!' said the officer who was showing them round. 'Sometimes it seems as if she's never going to stop heeling over to one side – it feels as if she's going to go right down below the water before she rights herself a bit, and then rolls back and over to the other side! Ah, you want to be in a bit of a gale on this ship.'

'I wish I could be,' said Mike. 'I'd like that.'

'Well, what about tea?' asked the officer. 'It will be ready for you. I'll take you down to the dining-room in the lift.'

'In the *lift*?' echoed the children in astonishment. 'Is there really a lift on this ship?'

'Good gracious, yes – quite a lot,' said the officer,

and led them into a big lounge between the fore and aft decks. At each side there were lifts. The doors of one slid open, and the children gazed into what looked like a little room.

'What a big lift!' said Ann. They all stepped in and down they went, past one, two, three floors – and then stopped.

'Fancy going down and down in a lift inside a ship!' said Mike. 'How many floors down does this lift go?'

'Fourteen,' said the officer. 'And after that there's yet another lift that goes down into the bowels of the ship.'

'Oooh – what an enormous dining-room!' said Belinda, as they went from the lift into a great, empty room.

'Yes – it holds hundreds and hundreds of people,' said the officer. 'You should see it when it's full of diners – and the band is playing – and great mounds of food are being carried about all over the place!'

But the dining-room was empty now and silent. The officer led them to a table in an alcove, set ready for tea. 'Here you are,' he said. 'Tea on the *Queen Elizabeth* for you! I hope you'll enjoy it!'

The children gazed in awe at the tea. 'What's that?' asked Ann, pointing to a plate of snow-white slices of what she thought must be cake.

'Bread and butter!' said Mummy. 'They have white bread aboard ship and in America. You'll like it.'

They did! They couldn't believe it was only bread and butter. It looked so beautifully white! And the cakes were amazing – all sugary and creamy and the prettiest shapes.

Belinda looked towards what were like two oblong cakes in the middle of the table.

'What are those?' she said. 'Can I have a slice, Granny?'

'Yes,' said Granny, and cut her a big one. It was in layers of three colours – pink, yellow and brown.

'Eat it with a spoon,' said Granny.

'Why?' asked Belinda in surprise. 'I don't eat a slice of cake with a spoon, do I?'

But she picked up her spoon and broke off a piece of the cake. Her eyes opened wide and she rolled them round at Mike and Ann in delight. She swallowed her mouthful.

'It's *ice-cream* cake!' she said. 'Would you believe it – we've got two great big cakes of ice-cream all to ourselves! Are we meant to eat them all, Mummy?'

'You won't be able to,' said her mother, laughing. 'Isn't it lovely? They have an enormous amount of ice-cream in America, you know – and these big ships must make tons of it for their passengers.'

'I wish we were passengers then,' said Belinda. 'I *wish* we were going to America. Do they have ice-cream every single day like this? I wouldn't eat anything but that. Mummy, have some!'

Everyone laughed at Belinda. She made up her mind not to leave a single scrap of the ice-cream cakes – but alas, they were so rich that nobody could possibly manage more than one slice. It was very sad.

They were sorry when they had to leave the big *Queen*. 'She's beautiful,' said Mike, as they went down the gangway and then stopped to look up at her great steep sides. 'How I wish I could live in her when she's really out on the sea!'

'Yes – she doesn't somehow seem like a real ship when she's here in dock,' said Mummy. 'But out at sea, when she's rolling and tossing – ah, that would be a wonderful thing!'

Mike and Belinda stood still to have one last look. 'I'm afraid it will be a long time before we see you again!' said Belinda, to the big ship. 'A very, very long time!'

But it wasn't. Surprising things were going to happen to Mike, Belinda and Ann!

4

It Can't Be True!

The three children went back to school again the next week, full of their visit to the *Queen Elizabeth*. The boys and girls listened, and wished they had gone too, especially when they heard about the marvellous lifts and the wonderful ice-cream cake.

Then, when Mike, Belinda and Ann went home the next Friday, what a surprise they had! Daddy was home before them, his face one big smile. Mummy was smiling too, and looked very excited indeed!

'Why is Daddy home so early?' asked Mike. 'And why do you look so excited, Mummy?'

'We were waiting to ask you something,' said Mummy. 'It's this – how would you all like to sail away on the *Queen Elizabeth*, and spend two weeks in New York?'

There wasn't a sound from the three children. They stared as if they couldn't have heard right. Mike opened and shut his mouth like a goldfish.

'Tongue-tied!' said Daddy, with a laugh. 'Say something, one of you, or you'll most certainly burst!'

Then all three yelled at the same time.

'Do you really mean it?'

'Is it really true?'

'When do we GO?'

Ann flung herself on her father. 'Tell us about it, Daddy. It isn't a joke, is it?'

'No,' said Daddy. 'It's quite true. The man who was going is ill – and so the firm have asked me to go instead. I'm allowed to take Mummy – and Granny says she will pay part of your fares if I like to take you as well for the trip.'

'She says it would do you a lot of good to see America – it will be like living in a geography lesson,' said Mummy. 'What do you think of that?'

'Mummy! I can't believe it,' said Mike. 'When do we go? And what about school?'

'You'll have to miss school for two or three weeks, I'm afraid,' said Mummy. 'But it will really be a great experience for you – a real education! Fancy Granny saying you ought to go – and helping to pay for you!'

'Good old Granny,' said Belinda. 'She's the kindest person in the world – except you and Daddy!'

'You still haven't said when we *go*,' said Mike.

'We go when the *Elizabeth* comes back,' said Mummy. 'She will be back here again next week. She's at New York now – and she leaves there tonight or tomorrow morning. We shall sail next Friday, or very early the next morning rather.'

'Next Friday!' said Belinda, her eyes shining.

'Next *Friday*! We'll have to come back home to the caravans then.'

'Yes – you must come home on Wednesday,' said Mummy. 'Then I can get your clothes and things ready, and pack. We have to be on board Friday night.'

'Shall we have to go to bed on board while she's in Southampton?' asked Mike. 'I would have liked to see her slipping out of the port by daylight. Shan't we see her leaving England?'

'Don't look so solemn!' said Mummy. 'The *Queen* has to be guided by the tide. You'll be fast asleep when she leaves – and you'll wake up to find her far out at sea in the morning!'

'And we shan't see land again for days!' said Belinda.

'Oh yes, you will,' said her mother. 'The *Elizabeth* goes to Cherbourg in France before she goes to America – so you'll see land the very next day.'

'Oh – shall we see France too, then?' asked Ann, in delight. 'Can we go ashore?'

'Dear me, no,' said Daddy. 'We shall probably stay outside Cherbourg, and watch the little steamers chugging out from the port with new passengers for the *Elizabeth*. You can watch that. You'll like it.'

'I can't believe it's true,' sighed Belinda. 'I thought last Saturday was wonderful enough – having tea on board – but *next* Saturday we'll be sailing over the ocean in the biggest ship in the world.'

'Can I take my doll Josephine?' asked Ann. 'It

would be an education for her too.'

Daddy laughed. 'Yes – you take her – she shall meet the American dolls and see how she likes them. Some of them don't only go to sleep, and talk, but they can walk too. We'll see what Josephine says to that.'

The children could hardly do any lessons at all the next week. They kept thinking of the *Queen Elizabeth*, and seeing her great red funnels towering high above her spotless decks.

'I know I shall get lost on such a big ship,' said Ann to Belinda. 'It's as big as a small town! I'll never know my way about.'

'We'll soon get used to it,' said Belinda. 'Did you know there was a swimming-pool, Ann? We couldn't see it when we went, because it was shut up – but there is one. We can go swimming in it.'

'Don't tell me any more,' begged Ann. 'It's beginning to sound like a fairy-tale – and I do want it to be true.'

It was true, of course. Wednesday came, and the children caught the bus to go home to the caravans.

'We've come!' cried Ann, seeing her mother waiting at the gate. 'It's Wednesday at last.'

'And soon it will be Friday,' said Mike. 'Only one more day – then Friday!'

Thursday was a busy day of washing clothes and packing lots of things. Ann wouldn't let her doll be packed. 'No – she wants to *see* everything,' she said. 'I'll carry her, Mummy.'

Thursday night came – the last to be spent in the caravans for some time. Then Friday morning dawned, fair and bright – a really lovely October day.

'It's Friday, it's Friday!' sang the three children as soon as they woke up. It didn't take them long to get dressed *that* day!

'We must say goodbye to Davey and Clopper,' said Ann. So they went to find the two horses and hugged them.

'We're going to America,' said Ann. 'But we'll come back. Goodbye, Davey, goodbye, Clopper. Be good, and I *might* perhaps send you a postcard!'

5

On Board at Last!

Granny lent them her car again, to drive down to Southampton. She didn't come with them because there wasn't room for her and all the luggage too. As it was, the children had to sit with suitcases all round their feet!

'Have you got our tickets, Daddy?' asked Ann, anxiously. 'Shall we get there in time? Suppose we have a puncture? Will the boat wait for us?'

'We'll be all right,' said Daddy. 'Yes, I've got the tickets, and I know which cabins we've got and everything.'

It didn't really seem very long before they were in Southampton again. Daddy took them to a little hotel to have supper. It was all very exciting.

They could hardly eat anything. Mike was anxious to go. 'We might be too late to get on,' he said. 'We really ought to go.'

'Mike – the boat doesn't sail till about half-past one at *night*,' said Daddy. 'Or rather, in the very early morning, long before dawn, while it's still pitch-dark.'

'Oh,' said Mike, and decided to eat something after all.

'Shall we be seasick?' said Ann, suddenly.

'Not a bit,' said Mummy, at once. 'And if you are, it soon passes. Now do eat that pudding, Ann.'

At last they were at the dock again, and at last they were walking up the gangway. But this time there seemed to be hundreds and hundreds of people walking on too! The children stared at them in wonder.

'Are they all going to America?' said Mike.

'Most of them,' said Daddy. 'Some are just going to see their friends off, of course. The ship looks different now, doesn't she, since the Saturday we saw her with hardly anyone on board?'

She did look different. It was night now and there were lights everywhere. The round portholes glittered like hundreds of eyes, and there was such a noise that Mike had to shout to hear himself speak.

'Keep close to me,' said Daddy. 'Our cabins are together, so we shall be all right once we've found them.'

They did find them at last. Belinda looked at them in awe. They were quite big, and had beds, not bunks. The big round porthole looked out over the dock, and she saw thousands of twinkling lights out there. She imagined what it would be like when she looked out in a day or two's time and saw nothing but sea.

'There's every single thing you want,' said Mike, looking round his mother's cabin. 'Wash-basin – dressing-table – wardrobe – drawers – and look, when you put this flap down, Mummy, it makes a little desk for you to write on!'

The three children had a cabin with three beds in. They were delighted. 'Can I have the one by the port-hole?' begged Belinda. 'Oh Mike, do let me. I want to be able to stand on the bed and look out of the port-hole any time in the night that I wake up.'

'Well, you won't see anything if you do,' said Mike. He looked longingly at the bed by the porthole. He badly wanted it himself, but he was very unselfish with his two sisters.

'All right,' he said, with a sigh. 'You can have the bed by the porthole going to America, Belinda, and Ann can have it coming back.'

'I don't want a bed by the porthole,' said Ann. 'I don't like to be as near the sea as that. I'm afraid it might leak in on me.'

'You're silly,' said Mike, cheering up. 'Well, if that's what you're afraid of, you can have the inside bed each time. I'll have the porthole bed coming back from America.'

A nice bright face with twinkling eyes popped round the door. 'Ah – I've got three children in this cabin of mine this time, have I? That's nice.'

The children stared at her. She looked very nice

and crisp and clean – rather like a nurse, the children thought. She laughed at their faces.

'I'm your stewardess,' she said. 'I look after you. If ever you want me, just ring that bell over there – and I'll come trotting along to see which of you is sick, or wants a hot-water bottle, or some more to eat!'

The children laughed. They liked this stewardess. 'Would you like something to eat now?' she said. 'I expect you've had your supper, haven't you? But would you like some nice sugary biscuits, and a big glass of creamy milk each – or some orange juice?'

All this sounded very nice. 'I'd love the biscuits and some orange juice,' said Belinda and the others said the same. Then Mummy came in, and smiled to hear that they had ordered eats and drinks already!

She began to unpack a few things for them. She laid their night things on the beds and set out their tooth-brushes and washing things.

'You behave exactly as if you were at home,' she said. 'Cleaning your teeth, washing, brushing your hair and everything.'

'And saying our prayers,' said Ann. 'I'm going to ask God to keep us safe when we're on the deep sea. I'd like him to keep a special lifeboat for me if anything happens.'

'You've got a special lifeboat already,' said Mummy. 'I'll show you yours tomorrow. And in that cupboard you've each got a special cork life jacket. You will have to learn how to put it on tomorrow.'

Belinda sighed. 'Everything is so lovely and exciting,' she said. 'Fancy having cork jackets of our own, too. I shall love to put mine on.'

'Now you must go to bed,' said Mummy. 'It's long past your bedtime. And here comes your nice stewardess with biscuits and orange-juice – and what biscuits!'

They certainly were wonderful ones. The three children hurriedly undressed, cleaned their teeth, washed, and brushed their hair, and hopped into bed.

'I shall say my prayers last of all,' said Ann. 'Then I can say thank you for these biscuits too. Oh dear – I'm sure I shall never go to sleep tonight!'

'I'm going to keep awake,' said Mike. 'I want to hear the anchor come up – and hear the fussy little tugs pulling away at the big *Queen* to get her out to sea. I want to feel her moving as she leaves Southampton.'

'Oh, so do I!' cried Belinda. But she and Ann fell fast asleep. Only Mike lay awake, waiting.

6

Goodbye to England

More and more passengers came on board the big ship, and found their different cabins. Cranes worked busily and loaded the enormous holds with luggage. There was a great deal of noise and bustle and excitement.

Belinda and Ann slept through it all. They were tired out with excitement. Mike kept awake for two hours, and then he felt his eyelids closing because they were so heavy. He propped them up with his fingers.

But then his fingers felt heavy, and slid down from his eyes. His eyes closed. He slept too. Poor Mike – he had so much wanted to be awake when the time came for the *Elizabeth* to leave the big port of Southampton.

Half-past one came. The tide was right. Little tugs fussed up in the darkness, and ropes were thrown from the big ship over to them. How was it possible for such tiny tugs to move such an enormous ship?

But they did. Gradually the *Queen Elizabeth* moved away from the dock-side. Gradually she left Southampton docks behind.

Mike awoke with a jump. He felt a peculiar movement far below him. He sat up, wondering what it was. Then he knew! The *Queen Elizabeth* was moving!

'She's away!' he thought and got out of bed. He groped his way to Belinda's bed, which was by the big porthole. He wondered if he would wake her if he stood up on her bed and looked out.

He cautiously got up on the bed. Belinda woke at once. 'Who is it?' she said, in a frightened voice. 'Where am I?'

'Sh! It's me, Mike! Belinda – the *Elizabeth* is moving! I felt her just now. Can *you* feel her? She's not keeping still any more. You can feel the water running under her!'

Belinda was thrilled. She knelt up to the porthole and the two of them looked out. They whispered together.

'Yes – we've left the dock-side. We must be right in the middle of the harbour. Look at all the lights slipping past.'

'Doesn't the water look a long long way down?' said Mike. 'And so awfully black! And look at all the lights twinkling in it, reflected from the dock-side.'

'Now she's left the dock,' said Belinda. 'Is she going backwards, Mike? She must be, to get out of the dock. Soon we shall feel her stopping – and then going the other way, shan't we?'

Belinda was quite right. The *Elizabeth* stopped when she was well out of the dock, and then began to move the other way. The little tugs hooted in farewell and chugged off by themselves. They had done their job.

'There goes a little tug,' said Mike, seeing one dimly in the starlit darkness. 'Aren't they clever, Belinda, the way they push and pull, and get a big ship like this safely out of the docks? I wouldn't mind having a tug of my own.'

'Now we're really going,' said Belinda, softly. 'I suppose we'll keep along the coast a bit – but by the time morning comes we'll be out of sight of land.'

'Till we reach France,' said Mike. 'And then we'll be days on the enormous Atlantic Ocean, hundreds of miles from anywhere.'

They were silent. The *Elizabeth* was big – but the ocean was vast. Belinda shivered a little. Then she thought of the big lifeboats and the life jacket and felt more cheerful. She watched the line of far-off lights that gradually passed behind them as the big ship ploughed on through the dark waters.

'I like to feel we're really moving, don't you, Mike?' said Belinda. 'I like the little rolls the ship gives now and again when a bigger wave than usual passes under her. Isn't this *fun*?'

The cabin door opened cautiously, and light streamed in from the passage outside. The two children looked round. They saw Mummy outlined in the doorway.

'Mummy!' said Belinda, in a loud whisper. 'Mummy, we've left Southampton now – did you know? We're off to America!'

'Sh!' said Mummy. 'You'll wake Ann. I wondered if you two were awake. Yes, we're really on our way now. I hope you didn't keep awake all the time.'

'No,' said Belinda. 'I only woke about twenty minutes ago.'

'Well, cuddle down into bed again now,' said Mummy. 'I won't stay in case I wake Ann. Mike, get back to your bed, dear.'

'Right,' said Mike and slipped down from Belinda's bed. 'Mummy, will you come and fetch us in the morning? We wouldn't know how to find the dining-room.'

'Of course I'll come,' said Mummy. 'Now, good-night, dears. Go to sleep at once.'

The door shut. Mike yawned. He really felt very sleepy indeed. He called softly to Belinda. 'Good-night, Belinda!'

But there was no answer. Belinda had curled up and was already fast asleep!

They all slept very soundly indeed in their comfortable little beds. They were awakened by a loud knocking on the door. Belinda woke in a fright, and sat up. She felt sure the boat must be sinking or something!

Then the stewardess put her head round the door, smiling. 'Sleepyheads, aren't you? This is the third time I've been along. Your mother says, will you get up now, because she will be ready to take you down to breakfast in ten minutes' time.'

'Oooh yes,' said Mike, scrambling out of bed. 'What's for breakfast, stewardess? Do you know?'

'Porridge, cereals, iced melon, stewed fruit, bacon, eggs, steak, fish, omelettes, chops, ham, tongue . . .' she began.

The children stared at her in amazement. 'Do we *have* to eat all that?' asked Mike.

The stewardess laughed. 'You can choose whatever you want, eat as much as you like, and take as long over it as you wish!' she said. 'So hurry up now, and get down to a really fine breakfast!'

They certainly did hurry up – and when Mummy came for them, they were all ready. Down in the lift they went to the enormous dining-room – and found their table. And when the menu came, the children simply didn't know what to choose from the dozens and dozens of things on it!

'If all the meals are like this, I *am* going to enjoy this trip!' said Mike.

7

A Wonderful Ship

That first day on the *Queen Elizabeth* was simply marvellous to the three children. At first they wouldn't go anywhere without their mother or father, because they really were afraid of getting lost!

'Everything's so *big*,' said Belinda. 'The decks are miles and miles long. It takes ages to go all round the ship on just one deck!'

They went to see the big swimming-pool, and Mummy said they might bathe there some time. They went to see the beautiful library with hundreds and hundreds of books waiting to be read. They found the children's corner there, and each of them borrowed a book to read.

'Though goodness knows when we'll have time to read a book on this lovely ship!' said Mike.

There were shops on the *Queen Elizabeth* too! The children went to look at them – all kinds of shops that sold anything the passengers wanted. How odd to have shops on a ship!

It was great fun up on the sports deck. It was windy up there, and the children had to hold on to their hats.

They went to watch the grown-ups playing games.

There were games with rope rings. There were games with great wooden discs that had to be pushed very hard indeed with a big wooden pusher. That was called shuffle-board. The children waited till the grown-ups had finished playing with the shuffle-board, and then they had a try.

But they couldn't push the great wooden counters very far! They tried their hand at throwing the rope rings on to numbered squares, and Mike was so good at that, that Daddy had a game with him. Mike nearly won!

'It's nice up here on the sports deck,' said Belinda, her cheeks glowing with the strong breeze. 'It isn't all enclosed with glass windows like the other decks down below – you can really taste the spray up here, and feel the wind. I like it.'

The great sea spread out round them for miles. Always there was the plash-plash-plash of waves against the ship's sides – a lovely sound. She left behind her a long white trail of foaming water.

'That's called the wake,' said Daddy. So they watched the wake forming behind the ship, spreading away as far as they could see.

'The fishes must be very astonished when a big ship like this comes by,' said Belinda, looking down into the water.

'I should be frightened if *I* were a fish and I suddenly

saw a great thing like this coming towards me,' said Ann. 'I should swim away quickly.'

'We're going fast now, aren't we, Daddy?' said Mike.

Daddy nodded. 'Yes – she's a fast ship, the *Elizabeth*. So is her sister, the *Queen Mary*.'

At eleven o'clock they went downstairs and found their own deck-chairs on the deck below. Mummy said that it was about time that deck stewards brought round little cups of hot soup and biscuits for everyone.

'Good gracious!' said Belinda. 'Do we really have hot soup in the middle of the morning? I do think this is a ship with good ideas!'

Sure enough the stewards appeared with trays of hot steaming soup in little bowls. There were biscuits to go with it. It was simply delicious. The children wondered if they might have another helping each, but Mummy said no.

'You will want to have an enormous lunch at one o'clock,' she said. 'Don't spoil it! It will take you about ten minutes to read all down the menu!'

After that they went to see the gym, where people were doing all kinds of exercises. There was a peculiar-looking imitation horse there, and Mike got on it. Up came the instructor, pulled a handle – and dear me, that horse came alive and began to do such extraordinary things that Mike nearly fell off! He clutched it hard round the neck and tried to stop himself slipping. Belinda and Ann screamed with laughter.

The horse bucked and reared and rocked from side to side till Mike yelled for mercy. He was very glad when it stopped and he was able to get off. Belinda got on and had a turn, but Ann wouldn't. She was quite certain she would fall off at once.

'This is a wonderful ship,' said Mike, happily. 'There's simply *everything* here – it's like a small town all neatly put together with everything anyone can want.'

They went up on the sports deck again after a lunch that was good enough to eat in a king's palace. 'Even the menu is like a book!' said Belinda, marvelling at the wonderful coloured cover. 'And look at the inside! Mummy, can we *really* choose any of these dishes? I simply don't know what to have.'

'I'm beginning with iced melon – then chicken soup – and two little chops with tomatoes and onions and mushrooms – and an ice-cream called Bombe-something,' said Ann, unexpectedly. 'And I think I'll finish up with iced melon too!'

It really took quite a long time deciding what they were going to have, but nobody seemed in a hurry at all. 'After all, no one's got a train or a bus to catch,' said Mike. 'There's all day long to choose food and games and wander round.'

They all felt rather full after such a marvellous

meal, and went up on the sports deck in the wind. It was nice up there. The sun shone, the sky was blue, and the sea was very blue too. Ann sat down in a corner and fell fast asleep!

She was awakened by a most terrible noise. She leapt up in a fright, yelling for her mother. 'Mummy, Mummy, what is it? Are we sinking? Have we hit a rock?'

But it was only the siren of the *Queen Elizabeth* hooting loudly because she was coming near France. It was such a sudden and tremendous noise that everyone looked startled for a moment.

'There's France!' Mike told Ann. 'Daddy says that port is Cherbourg. We're not going right into the harbour because it's a bit rough here. So they're sending out boats to us with new passengers, and taking off passengers that want to go to France.'

Out came two little steamers from Cherbourg, and the *Queen Elizabeth* stayed quite still, waiting.

'Isn't it fun?' said Mike, leaning over the sports-deck rail to watch. 'How small those steamers look! I'm glad I belong to the *Queen Elizabeth*. It makes me feel very important!'

8

Out on the Ocean

That first day seemed deliciously long and full of excitement and surprises. They were all very tired when they went to bed. The *Elizabeth* had left the coast of France, and was now on her way to America! The sea wasn't quite so smooth and calm, and sometimes the children staggered a little as they walked down the passage to their cabin.

'One day gone,' said Mike. 'I hope the days don't go *too* quickly! I wonder what we do tomorrow. It will be Sunday. How can we go to church? I haven't seen a church here, have you?'

'You couldn't build a church on a ship,' said Ann. 'We'll have to see what happens.'.

Mummy told them the next morning that there were two things that day that she wanted them to do.

'There is a church service at eleven o'clock,' she said, 'and you must put on your hats and coats just as if you were going to a real church, although the service is only being held in the big lounge. You must each take pennies for a collection too.'

'Fancy going to church on a ship!' said Ann. 'I do

like that. What's the second thing we have to go to, Mummy?'

'Lifeboat drill,' said Mummy. 'We all have to get out our life jackets from the cupboards in our cabins and put them on properly. Then we have to go up to our boat stations . . .'

'Boat stations! Are there stations here, then?' asked Mike. 'I haven't seen them!'

'They're not really *stations*,' said Mummy. 'Just places where we meet for lifeboat drill – or to get our lifeboat if there was any need to.'

'How do we know which is our boat-station?' asked Belinda.

Mummy showed her some directions on a card in the cabin. 'This shows you the way to yours,' she said. 'Up the stairs, and up again. On to that deck. And go to the place on the deck marked with your number. It's quite easy. There are many different stations, and each passenger must know his own.'

'So that if the boat was wrecked, we'd all know where to go at once, and be helped into our life-boats, I suppose,' said Mike. 'That's very sensible.'

They went to church service at eleven o'clock, looking very proper in hats and coats. Ann even put her gloves on.

It was very like a real church service except that there were no proper pews, only chairs, and it seemed extraordinary to look out of the windows and see miles of green-blue sea outside instead of houses and streets.

Ann was very pleased with one hymn that ended each verse with:

Oh, hear us when we cry to Thee
For those in peril on the sea.

'That's a very good hymn to sing on a ship,' she said afterwards. 'I'm glad there's a hymn that prays for people on the sea.'

The captain gave a short, interesting little sermon, and everyone listened. There were more hymns and prayers and a collection. Belinda thought it was the nicest church service she had ever been to in her life. It was peculiar to feel the ship moving all the time, and to see the white clouds racing by as the ship moved along.

'Now for lifeboat drill,' said Mummy, and took them to their cabin to get their life jackets. A loud bell rang out and made them jump.

'That's to warn everyone to go to their lifeboat stations,' said Mummy. 'If ever we hear that in the middle of the night, up we must get, snatch at our life jackets and run to our stations as fast as ever we can.'

This sounded very exciting, but none of the children wanted it to happen!

They got their life jackets and Mummy showed them

how to tie them round them. They began to laugh.

'We look *enormous*!' said Mike. 'Do look at Ann. She's as broad as she's long!'

'Hurry up,' said Mummy. 'This is a thing we always have to be quick about, even if it's only practice.'

Soon they all had their life jackets on, and Mummy and Daddy took them to the deck where their boat-station was. About fifty people were with them. Farther along there were other groups of people. Every passenger had his own boat-station, and now he knew where to go for it.

'And, you see, in a real emergency, when the life-boats are lowered for us to get into,' said Daddy, 'everyone gets into his own lifeboat, and there are just the right number. Then down the boat goes into the sea, and is cast off to safety.'

'All the same, I hope it won't happen,' said Ann, looking rather scared.

'No, it won't,' said Mummy. 'But it's good to know what we must do if it *should* happen.'

When everyone was at his boat-station, an officer came up to Daddy's group. He went round to see that everyone's life jacket was on properly. Then he talked to them all, and told them exactly what to do if the ship met with an accident.

The children were glad to go back to their cabins and take off their bulky life jackets. 'Is it dinner-time yet?' asked Ann. 'I had an enormous breakfast, and soup and biscuits at half-past ten, and now I feel hungry all over again.'

'I suppose you'll start off with iced melon again?' said Mike, with a grin. 'So far, you've begun every single meal with iced melon. You'll turn into a melon yourself if you go on like this.'

'And do you know what *you'll* turn into?' said Ann, as they went to get into the lift to go down to the big dining-room. 'You'll turn into a chocolate ice-cream – and you'll be lucky if I don't eat you!'

9

A Gale Blows Up

The days began to slip away, but on the fourth day things suddenly changed. Great clouds came over the sea, and huge waves began to form in the strong wind that blew.

Then the *Queen Elizabeth* showed that, big or not, she was a ship that took notice of big waves! She began to roll from side to side. First this side a little, then back to the other side.

The children began to stagger a little as they went about the ship, which they now knew very well indeed. 'I hope she doesn't roll any farther over,' said Mike. 'I'm not sure I like it very much.'

'Why? Do you feel sick?' asked Ann.

'No. But I just don't *want* her to roll any farther over,' said Mike. However, she took no notice of Mike's wishes, and began to roll more than ever.

When night came ropes had been put up on the decks so that people might hold on to them as they went. The children were quite glad when bedtime came. At least their beds felt firm and safe!

But it was most peculiar to lie on a bed that slanted

sideways when the ship rolled! 'I feel as if I ought to hold on to the sides in case I fall out,' said Ann.

When the light was out, it seemed as if the ship's rolling felt worse than ever. Down – down – down – to one side, until the children really thought they must be touching the water – then up, up, up, and over to the other side – down – down – down again, lower and lower till Ann sat up.

'I don't like it,' she wailed. 'Suppose it rolled so far over that it didn't come back!'

The stewardess put her head round the door. 'Who's this shouting out?' she said, and switched on the light. 'Dear me, surely you're not making a fuss about a bit of a gale like this? You want to be in a *real* storm to have something worth shouting about!'

'Isn't this a real storm, then?' asked Ann.

'Good gracious no. It'll be gone by the morning,' said the stewardess. 'A big ship always rolls a bit in a gale – she can't help it. But you want to be out in a small boat to know what pitching and tossing and rolling are really like!'

All the children were relieved to feel that there wasn't much likelihood of the alarm bell's sounding for them to put on life jackets, rush to their boat-stations and get into a lifeboat!

'Now you just listen to what I say,' said the stewardess. 'The gale's beginning to die down even now – we're only touching the fringe of the storm and we'll soon be out of it. You must enjoy the rolling instead of getting scared of it! You want a ship to behave like a ship, don't you?'

She said goodnight and went. 'Well, we shall certainly have something to tell the children at school about when we get back home,' said Mike, sleepily. 'I'm going to pretend I'm in a rocking-bed and enjoy it!'

'So am I,' said Belinda. 'That's a good idea.'

Ann didn't say anything. She had suddenly remembered something. What did a storm matter? What did a rolling ship matter? Hadn't she prayed to God that very night to keep them all safe – and here she was thinking He couldn't manage to protect them in even a *little* gale!

'That's very bad of me, and very untrusting,' she thought. 'I'm not afraid any more now.' And she fell asleep thinking of the hymn they had sung on Sunday, which now seemed an even more sensible hymn than ever,

> Oh, hear us when we cry to Thee
> For those in peril on the sea.

The stewardess was right. The *Elizabeth* sailed right out of the gale by the morning, and when the children woke up, what a difference! The big ship hardly rolled at all – all the guide-ropes had been taken down – and people who had felt seasick came down to make a good breakfast.

And now the great excitement was the arrival at New York! The gale had slowed down the *Elizabeth,* and instead of arriving that night she would not arrive till ten o'clock the next morning.

'Which will be very nice,' said Daddy, 'because you will be able to watch the coastline all the way up the big river to New York. And we shall pass something that the Americans are very proud of – the colossal Statue of Liberty, holding a great torch aloft.'

'All the same – I feel quite sad now to think we're going to leave the *Queen Elizabeth,*' said Belinda, looking solemn. 'I've got used to her, and I love her.'

'Well, we're going *back* in her, in two or three weeks' time, aren't we?' said Mike. 'You'll have another trip just like this.'

'Except that the clocks will have to be put forward each day, instead of back,' said Mummy. That had been a very funny thing to happen, the children thought.

Every day their clocks had been set back an hour, because they were travelling westwards, so they had gained an hour in their day. But when they returned eastwards they would lose an hour each day – the clocks would be set an hour forward! It seemed funny to meddle about with time like that – but, as they already knew, the time in New

York wasn't the same as the time in England at that particular moment!

They were all excited to see land again. They passed into the great river and watched the enormous buildings on each side. 'Much, much bigger than ours,' said Mike.

'You wait till you see some of the high buildings in New York!' said Daddy. 'You won't believe your eyes!'

'There's the Statue of Liberty!' said somebody, suddenly, and everyone craned their necks to see the enormous and magnificent statue, guarding the entrance to New York harbour. Only the stewards did not bother to look – they had seen New York before.

'America at last!' said Mike, excited. 'The newest country in the world – and one of the finest! When do we land, Daddy? I can hardly wait!'

But he had to wait, of course, and at last their turn came to walk down the gangway and on to American soil.

'America!' said Ann, holding up her doll Josephine. 'Take a look, Josephine – you've come halfway across the world – and now we're in America!'

10

America at Last

New York was a most extraordinary city to Mike, Belinda and Ann. They stepped off the *Elizabeth* and marvelled to see how the big ship stretched herself right over the street. Her huge bows rose above some of the buildings, and this looked very peculiar.

They took a large yellow taxi to their hotel. The taxi-driver spoke exactly like they had heard many people speak on the films.

'He said "twenny-foor" instead of "twenty-four",' whispered Ann to Mike. 'Like Mickey Mouse talks on the films. Is that the American language?'

The taxi drove very fast indeed, and whenever they came to red traffic lights it pulled up with a terrific jerk. Then all the taxis waiting began to hoot loudly without stopping.

'Oh dear,' said Mummy. 'Does this go on all the time?'

'You'll soon get so used to the noise of New York streets that you just won't notice it after a day or two,' said Daddy. 'Look, children – do you see those skyscrapers over there?'

They looked – and gasped. The buildings were so tall that they had to crane back their necks to see the tops of them as they raced past. Floor after floor after floor – however many storeys were there?

'You wanna see the Empire State Building,' said the taxi-driver, joining suddenly in the conversation. 'That's what you wanna see. Over a hundred floors. Yes, *sir*!'

'*Can* we, Daddy?' asked Mike, eagerly. 'Do we go up in a lift? Can we go to the very top?'

'You've got to take more than one lift if you wanna get to the top of the Empire State building,' said the taxi-driver. 'You go right to the top and have a looksee round. You'll see little old New York all right then, and a lot more too!'

Some of the streets were very dark because the walls of the very tall buildings rose opposite one another and kept out the sun. Lights burned in many of the windows in those streets, though it was full daylight.

'Why don't *we* build skyscrapers in London?' asked Belinda. 'It certainly does save a lot of space.'

'New York is built on hard rock,' said Daddy. 'It will bear tremendous weights. We couldn't build enormous buildings like this in London – they would gradually sink with their weight!'

'It's a very good name – skyscrapers,' said Ann. 'They do really look as if they must be scraping the sky, Daddy.'

'New York's not a *bit* like London,' said Mike. 'The streets are so wide and straight – and quite straight streets run off the main avenue. There aren't any winding streets, or higgledy-piggledy ones, as there are in London.'

'Ah, London grew, but New York was planned,' said Daddy. 'They are both beautiful in their own way. Now look, this is Broadway. At night the lights here – the advertisement signs – are wonderful. I'll bring you out to see them.'

They came to their hotel at last. It was a skyscraper too, though not a very big one. Mike looked at the number of floors marked on the lift – thirty-two! Goodness, no wonder the lift shot up at such a speed. It would take all day to go from the bottom to the top if it didn't go so quickly!

They unpacked their things and settled in. They thought their bedrooms were enormous after the ones on the *Elizabeth*. They looked out of the window and gave a gasp.

They were so high up that the people down in the road looked like ants! The children stared in amazement.

'Look at those cars!' said Mike. 'Honestly, they don't look as big as my dinky-cars at home!'

'No, they don't,' said Belinda. 'They just don't look real. They're so small they make me feel as if I must suddenly have become a giant – so that everyone looks tiny to me!'

'I don't like the feeling very much,' said Ann. 'Nor does Josephine. I shan't look out any more.'

Meals in America were enormous. The menus seemed even longer than those on the *Elizabeth*. The children gazed at them in astonishment, when they went down to a meal in the restaurant.

'Waffles! What are they?' asked Ann. 'They sound like the name for a rabbit or something. Hamburgers – Mummy, are they nice? And oh, look – hot-dogs! Can I have a hot-dog? Not if it's *really* dog, though. I wouldn't want to eat a dog.'

Everyone laughed. Ann looked round and her eyes opened wide when she saw the enormous platefuls of food that the waiters were setting in front of the guests.

'Have we got to eat so much?' she said to her mother. 'We had big helpings on the *Queen Elizabeth*, but these are even bigger.'

'I'll ask for small helpings for you,' said Mummy. So she did. But dear me, they were still so big that the children could do no more than nibble at them!

'Oh Mummy – will it all be wasted?' said Belinda, who knew how careful her mother was with food at home. 'What will happen to it?'

'It'll go into the pig-bucket, I expect,' said Mummy.

'The Americans waste far more than we eat – but it's America, and that's the way they like to live. I daresay if we had as much food as they had, we'd be the same!'

'Oh dear – I don't like to leave so much,' groaned Belinda, 'but I shall be ill if I eat all this.'

'English people no eat much,' said the waiter, taking her plate and smiling. He was an Italian American.

'Let's go out on Broadway now,' said Mike, looking out of the windows. 'It's dark. We could see the lights, Daddy. I'd like to do that.'

So out they went on Broadway to see one of the sights of the world – the masses of twinkling, racing, jigging, blazing, brilliant lights on all the tall buildings everywhere. What a sight it was.

'Better than fireworks on Bonfire Night!' said Ann. And it really was!

11

A Wonderful City

The Americans were very friendly. As soon as Daddy met the people he had come over to see, they asked to meet his little family.

They made a great fuss of the children, and said they had wonderful manners. Mummy thought secretly that they had much better manners than the American children, who spoke loudly and were often rude to grown-ups. She felt proud of her three.

Nobody could have been nicer or more generous than their friends in New York. Every day Mummy found fresh flowers in her room sent by one friend or another. If she was asked out to dinner a beautiful box would arrive, tied up with magnificent ribbon – and inside would be a lovely buttonhole or shoulder-spray of flowers.

The children were not forgotten either. 'Look,' squealed Ann, coming into her mother's room with a parcel she had undone. 'Did you EVER see such a box of sweets in your life! Mummy, LOOK!'

Mummy looked. So did the others. It was certainly magnificent. The box was covered with bits of ribbon made to look like flowers, and had a big sash of ribbon round it – far better than any hair-ribbon Ann had!

Inside were layers upon layers of wonderful sweets. 'Candies, the Americans call them,' said Mike. 'Oh, Ann – what a *magical* box. They look too good to be eaten.'

'Have one?' said Ann, and soon they were all eating the candies, which were certainly nicer than any they had ever had in their lives.

Belinda had a doll sent to her, and Mike had a wonderful pistol. It could shoot water, but if you fitted a bulb to the tip, it would light up like a torch when you pulled the trigger – and if you took out the bulb and put in a little paper of cartridges it would go off pop-pop-pop at top speed when the trigger was pulled.

Belinda's doll could walk. Belinda could hardly believe it when she saw it walk rather unsteadily over the floor, one foot after the other.

'Oh!' she cried, 'just look. She's far, far better than Josephine, Ann.'

'She's not,' said Ann, hugging Josephine. 'Anyway, I don't want Josephine to walk. Her legs aren't strong enough yet.'

Flowers, candies, fruit, chocolate, toys, books – everyone showered presents on the little English family. Surely there couldn't be more friendly or generous people in the world? Invitations poured down on them too – dinner-parties, afternoon parties, all kinds of parties. Mummy had to buy the children new clothes, because they really hadn't brought enough with them!

'I don't know *how* we're going to return all this friendliness,' said Daddy, in despair. 'The Americans are rich, and English people are poor – I haven't enough money to repay all this kindness.'

But the Americans didn't want any return. It was just their way. They liked Daddy and his family, and they wanted to show it.

The children lived in a whirl. There was hardly time to go sight-seeing at first. Mummy took them to see the shops, which were full of the most beautiful things in the world. She took them to a cake-shop too, and the children blinked when they saw the wonderful cakes. Were they real?

'It's *such* a pity, Mummy – I'd like to eat dozens of those cakes,' said Belinda, longingly, 'but when I've had one, I'm so full I can't eat any more. But American children can eat four or five at a time. I've seen them.'

'Well, I expect you enjoy your one as much as they enjoy their four or five,' said Mummy.

Another thing that the children found very strange was the number of people from many different cultures. Daddy said that because America was a much newer country than Britain, people had come from lots of other countries to make her their home. It was so interesting. They made many new friends.

The Afro-American woman who cleaned the corridor had twinkling eyes and dazzling white teeth.

'You been up to the top of the Empire State, honey?' said the friendly old cleaner. 'Tell your Ma to take you along!'

And so one day Mummy and Daddy took them to the Empire State Building, the highest in New York. It was so high that Ann felt sure it really did touch the clouds.

Up they went in the lifts, shooting skywards so quickly that Ann clutched her tummy.

'What's the matter?' asked Daddy, smiling. 'Have you left your tummy behind?'

'It felt like it, when we suddenly shot up,' said Ann. 'Oh Daddy – what a fast lift!'

The liftman spoke to them. 'Better look out for the pop in your ears now, sir,' he said. 'We're getting pretty high, and some people's ears go pop, and they feel funny. But it's nothing.'

Sure enough, their ears did go pop with a curious little noise in their ear drums. Ann felt a bit giddy, but it soon passed off.

They got into the last lift, to go up the top dozen or so floors. Up they went, and then, click! The door opened and they stepped out on top of the Empire State Building.

'OH!' cried Mike, in amazement. 'Mummy! We're right on the very top of the world!'

And really it did seem like it. Far, far below lay the earth, stretching out for miles and miles and miles all round the tower. An aeroplane flew by – below them! How extraordinary! People down in the far-off street were tiny dots – cars were smaller than even Mike's dinky-ones at home.

'What a building!' said Daddy. 'What a height! What a view!'

'We must be very near to Heaven up here,' said Ann, and the others smiled. Ann looked up as if she expected to see an angel or two around. But there was nothing but a few fleecy white clouds.

Then back they went down to earth again – down, down, down in the express lift, almost gasping at the way the lift seemed to fall down. Ann clutched her tummy again.

'I do like America,' said Belinda. 'It's full of the most wonderful things – it's *almost* magic!'

12

Time to go Home

Their time in America fled away fast. '*Every* thing goes fast in America; the taxis, the lifts, the parties – and even the time!' said Mike.

'Yes, no sooner is it morning than it seems to be night again,' said Belinda. 'I do really begin to wonder if time *is* different here – I mean, perhaps an hour isn't really an hour: perhaps it's only half an hour.'

'Oh, it's an hour all right,' said Mummy. 'It goes quickly because everything is strange and new and exciting, and the days go whizzing by.'

'I don't want to leave America,' said Ann. 'I like it.'

'Well, shall we leave you behind?' said Mummy. 'I've no doubt one of our American friends would love to keep a nice little girl like you.'

Ann looked alarmed. 'Oh *no*!' she said. 'It's just that I'm loving everything so much. I love England too. I couldn't *bear* not to go back.'

'I shan't mind going back at all,' said Mike. 'I love America and the Americans – but somehow they make me feel more English than ever, and they make me feel I belong to England. I want to get back to England, though I wouldn't mind staying a few weeks more here, Mummy.'

'Well, we've got our return tickets for home now,' said Mummy, 'and anyway we've very little money left to spend here. When the *Queen Elizabeth* docks in New York on Wednesday, off we go in her, back home!'

The last day or two Mummy spent shopping with the children. They wanted to take little presents home for all their friends. The difficulty was what to take!

'There are so many things to choose from,' said Belinda, looking round a big store in despair. 'I just can't make up my mind. I mean, there are *thousands* of things here I'd like to take back. Don't Americans have a lot of everything, Mummy?'

'They do,' said Mummy, 'but then America is a rich country. She can afford to have everything.'

'Next time we come, don't let's stay in New York all the time,' said Belinda. 'Let's go and stay somewhere in the country, Mummy. I want to see what the trees and the flowers are like – I've hardly seen a tree in New York! And I've hardly seen a dog either.'

'Yes, it would be nice to stay somewhere in the country,' said Mummy. 'After all, we haven't really seen much of America if we only stay in New York – any more than Americans would see much of England if they only stayed in London.'

'That's true,' said Belinda. 'England's made up of

a lot of things, isn't it, Mummy, not just towns. It's – well, it's primroses in springtime . . .'

'And taking the dogs for a long walk,' said Mike.

'And sailing down the river,' said Daddy.

'And watching the first green blades come through in the fields of corn,' said Mummy, 'and seeing all our lovely little patchwork of fields, with their odd shapes and sizes.'

'It's Davey and Clopper the horses,' said Mike, remembering suddenly.

'And treading on the first patches of ice when we go to school in the winter,' said Belinda.

'Oh do stop,' said Ann. 'I'm getting so dreadfully homesick. How could we *ever* have left England?'

'It's good to travel,' said Daddy. 'We see how other people live and make themselves happy – and we love our own home and country all the more for seeing other people's. Each of us loves his own country best, and his own home best and his own family best.'

'When are we going to pack?' demanded Ann. 'I suddenly feel I want to. Oh Daddy – think how pleased Davey and Clopper will be to see us again!'

'I wonder if the caravans are all right,' said Mummy. 'I wonder if . . .'

'What a lot of home-birds you are, all of a sudden,' said Daddy, but he looked pleased. 'Well, the *Queen Elizabeth* sails at midnight tomorrow, so you can begin to pack as soon as you like.'

They packed – and dear me, Daddy had to go out and spend some of his last precious dollars on a new suitcase, because they had so many presents there just wasn't room to pack them all in!

'I shall carry Sadie, my walking doll,' said Belinda.

'Better put a bit of string on her, or buy her some toy reins, then,' said Mike. 'She might walk overboard!'

They said goodbye to all the friends they had made. They promised to come again for a longer stay. They took a last look at the wonderful lights on Broadway. And then they taxied to the *Queen Elizabeth*, which had now arrived once more and was down at the docks, waiting for them.

'There she is!' cried Mike, as he saw her enormous bows sticking up over the street. 'Good old Lizzie!'

'British, not American,' said Belinda, proudly. 'Britain is very tiny compared with America, isn't it, Mummy? But even a small country can do grand things!'

'Of course,' said Mummy. 'Now, here we are – up the gangway you go!'

And up they went, the girls clutching Josephine and Sadie, and Mike carrying his marvellous pistol. What a surprise when they got to their cabins!

Their American friends were generous to the last. Great sprays of flowers were there with friendly messages, boxes of magnificent roses, beautiful buttonholes to wear at dinner the next night, boxes of candies for the children!

'What a people!' said Daddy, as he looked at the enormous collection. 'I wonder we can bear to leave America, and go back to England!'

But the little island far away across the ocean, set in its own silver sea, was their home – the home they loved and wanted.

'Speed the ship!' said Daddy, as at last the *Elizabeth* began to move. 'Speed the ship home!'

'Home to England, dear old England,' chanted the children. 'Speed the ship, Captain, speed the ship!'

And away went the great ship, ploughing through the waves, eager to get back to England – it was her own home too!